SHAKESPEARE ILLUSTRATED CLASSICS

# William Shakespeare's HAMLET

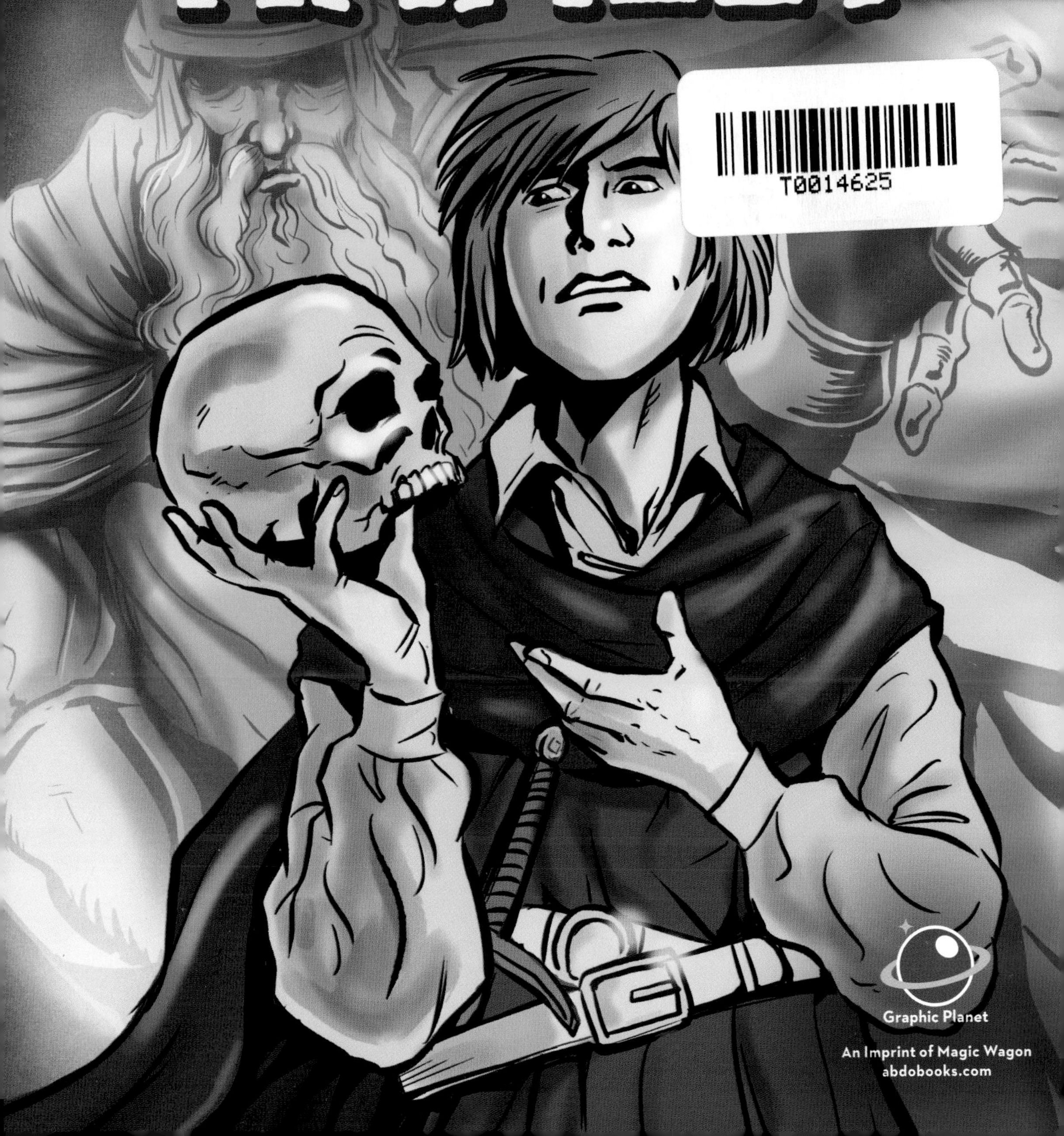



Graphic Planet
An Imprint of Magic Wagon
abdobooks.com

abdobooks.com

Published by Magic Wagon, a division of ABDO, PO Box 398166, Minneapolis, Minnesota 55439. Copyright © 2023 by Abdo Consulting Group, Inc. International copyrights reserved in all countries. No part of this book may be reproduced in any form without written permission from the publisher. Graphic Planet™ is a trademark and logo of Magic Wagon.

Printed in the United States of America, North Mankato, Minnesota.
052022
092022

Adapted by Rebecca Dunn
Cover art by Dave Shephard
Interior art by Ben Dunn
Edited by Tamara L. Britton and Tyler Gieseke
Interior layout and design by Candice Keimig and Colleen McLaren

**Library of Congress Control Number: 2021952001**

**Publisher's Cataloging-in-Publication Data**

Names: Shakespeare, William; Dunn, Rebecca, authors. | Dunn, Ben, illustrator.
Title:  William Shakespeare's Hamlet / by William Shakespeare, Adapted by Rebecca Dunn; illustrated by Ben Dunn.
Description: Minneapolis, Minnesota: Magic Wagon, 2023. | Series: Shakespeare illustrated classics
Summary: After the death of Denmark's King Hamlet, his ghost appears and tells his son, also called Hamlet, to avenge his wrongful death, which leads to more tragedy.
Identifiers: ISBN 9781098233273 (lib. bdg.) | ISBN 9781644948415 (pbk.) | ISBN 9781098234119 (ebook) | ISBN 9781098234539 (Read-to-Me ebook)
Subjects: LCSH:  Hamlet (Shakespeare, William)--Juvenile fiction. |  Hamlet (Legendary character)--Juvenile fiction. | Princes--Juvenile fiction. | Murder--Juvenile fiction. | Royal houses--Juvenile fiction. | Literature--Juvenile fiction.
Classification: DDC 741.5--dc23

# Table of Contents

# Cast of Characters

**HAMLET**
Prince of Denmark

**LAERTES**
Ophelia's brother

**OPHELIA**
Polonius's daughter

**LORD POLONIUS**
Father of Ophelia
and Laertes

**QUEEN GERTRUDE**
King Hamlet's widow,
Hamlet's mother

**REYNALDO**
Lord Polonius's
servant

**PRINCE
FORTINBRAS**
Prince of Norway

**HORATIO**
Friend of Hamlet

**MARCELLUS**
Officer

**KING CLAUDIUS**
New king of Denmark

**GUILDENSTERN**
Courtier

**ROSENCRANTZ**
Courtier

**VOLTEMAND**
Courtier

**CORNELIUS**
Courtier

**KING HAMLET'S
GHOST**

4

# Synopsis

*Hamlet* is a tragic Shakespearean tale of revenge. The story takes place in the 1400s or 1500s, a period known as the early Renaissance. Most of the play unfolds at the castle Elsinore, a seaside fort in the east part of Denmark. Denmark is a small European country on the Jutland peninsula and nearby islands.

King Hamlet has just died. Queen Gertrude is his widow, and his brother has just married the queen. He is now known as King Claudius. The two married to avoid the appearance that Denmark is weak. The threat of invasion looms as Prince Fortinbras of Norway seeks vengeance for his father's earlier death at the hands of King Hamlet. The title character, Prince Hamlet, is distraught at his own father's death and his mother's quick remarriage. Soon, the dead King Hamlet's ghost returns and tells young Hamlet he was murdered by Claudius, and the ghost instructs Hamlet to avenge his death.

To test the ghost's story, Hamlet hires traveling actors to perform a play. The play's plot is close to what the ghost says King Claudius has done. When Claudius appears angered and retreats from the play, Hamlet believes the ghost. That night, Queen Gertrude asks Hamlet to speak with her while Lord Polonius, a nobleman, is hidden and listening. Hamlet finds out and kills Polonius.

Claudius plans with Polonius's son, Laertes, to kill Hamlet and avenge the nobleman's death. Ophelia, who is Polonius's daughter and Hamlet's love, dies while grieving for her father. Laertes challenges Hamlet to a sword fight, and Claudius attempts to poison Hamlet. Many deaths ensue.

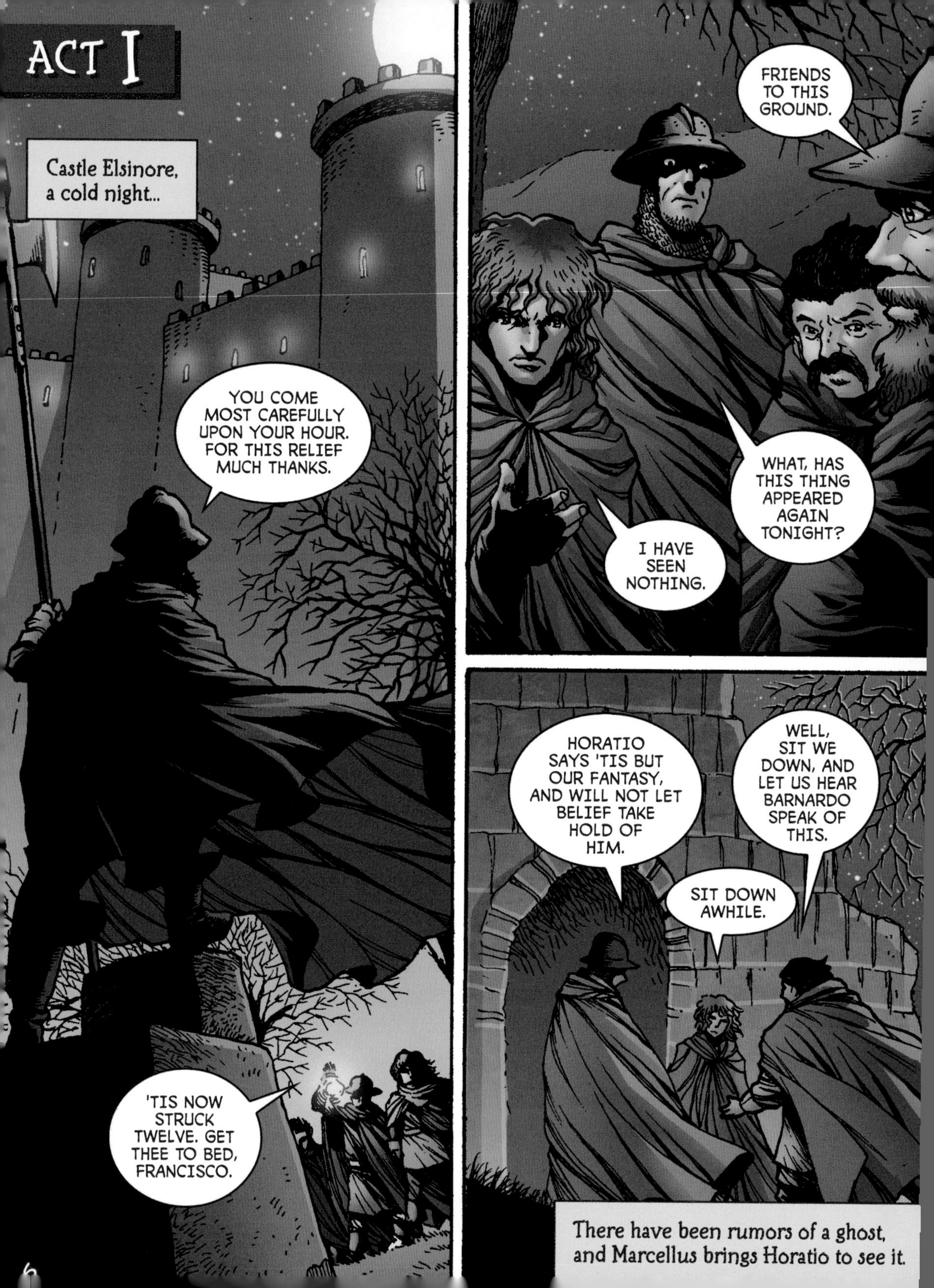
ACT I
Castle Elsinore, a cold night...
YOU COME MOST CAREFULLY UPON YOUR HOUR. FOR THIS RELIEF MUCH THANKS.
'TIS NOW STRUCK TWELVE. GET THEE TO BED, FRANCISCO.
FRIENDS TO THIS GROUND.
WHAT, HAS THIS THING APPEARED AGAIN TONIGHT?
I HAVE SEEN NOTHING.
HORATIO SAYS 'TIS BUT OUR FANTASY, AND WILL NOT LET BELIEF TAKE HOLD OF HIM.
SIT DOWN AWHILE.
WELL, SIT WE DOWN, AND LET US HEAR BARNARDO SPEAK OF THIS.
There have been rumors of a ghost, and Marcellus brings Horatio to see it.

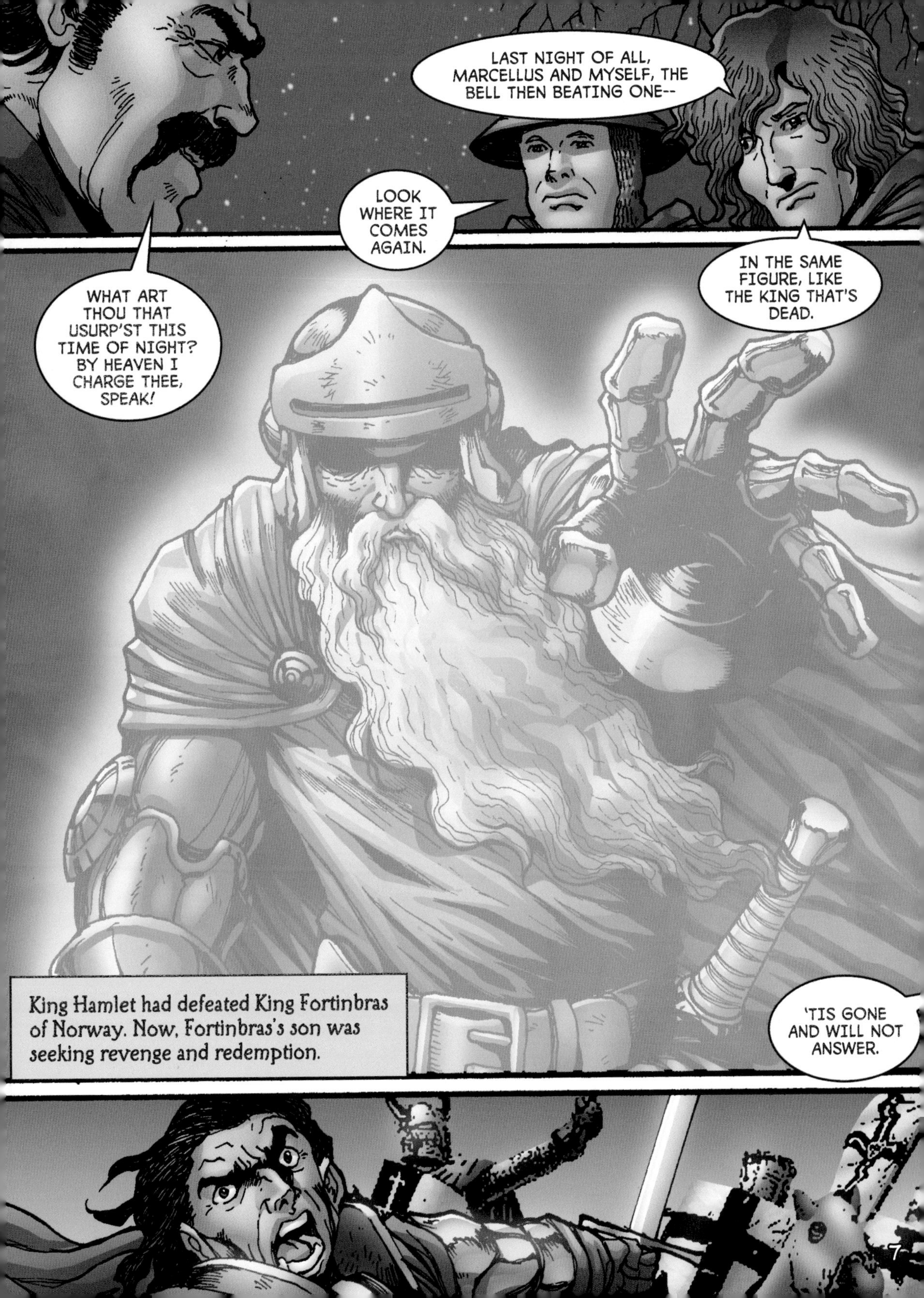
LAST NIGHT OF ALL, MARCELLUS AND MYSELF, THE BELL THEN BEATING ONE--
LOOK WHERE IT COMES AGAIN.
WHAT ART THOU THAT USURP'ST THIS TIME OF NIGHT? BY HEAVEN I CHARGE THEE, SPEAK!
IN THE SAME FIGURE, LIKE THE KING THAT'S DEAD.
King Hamlet had defeated King Fortinbras of Norway. Now, Fortinbras's son was seeking revenge and redemption.
'TIS GONE AND WILL NOT ANSWER.

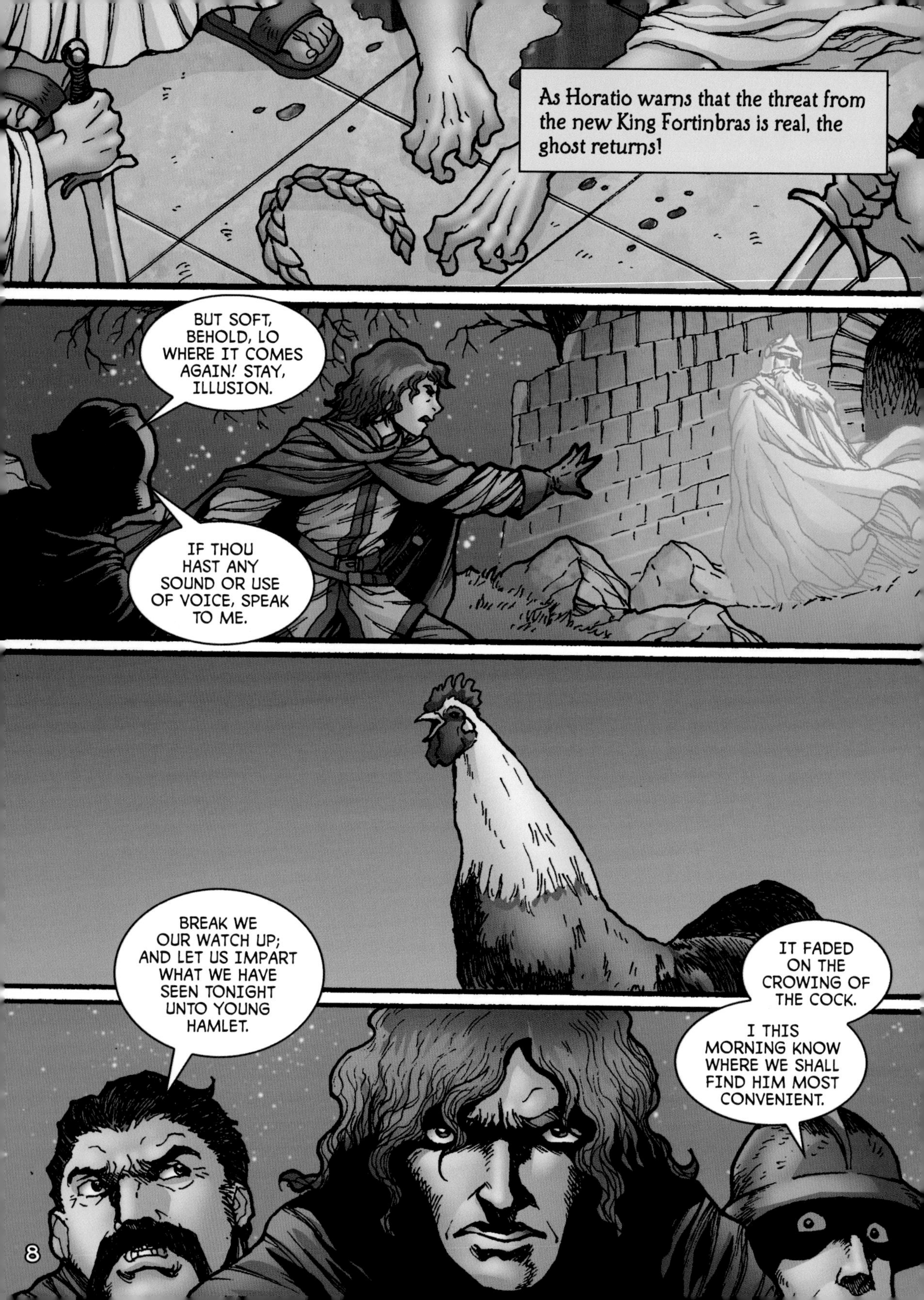
As Horatio warns that the threat from the new King Fortinbras is real, the ghost returns!
BUT SOFT, BEHOLD, LO WHERE IT COMES AGAIN! STAY, ILLUSION.
IF THOU HAST ANY SOUND OR USE OF VOICE, SPEAK TO ME.
BREAK WE OUR WATCH UP; AND LET US IMPART WHAT WE HAVE SEEN TONIGHT UNTO YOUNG HAMLET.
IT FADED ON THE CROWING OF THE COCK.
I THIS MORNING KNOW WHERE WE SHALL FIND HIM MOST CONVENIENT.

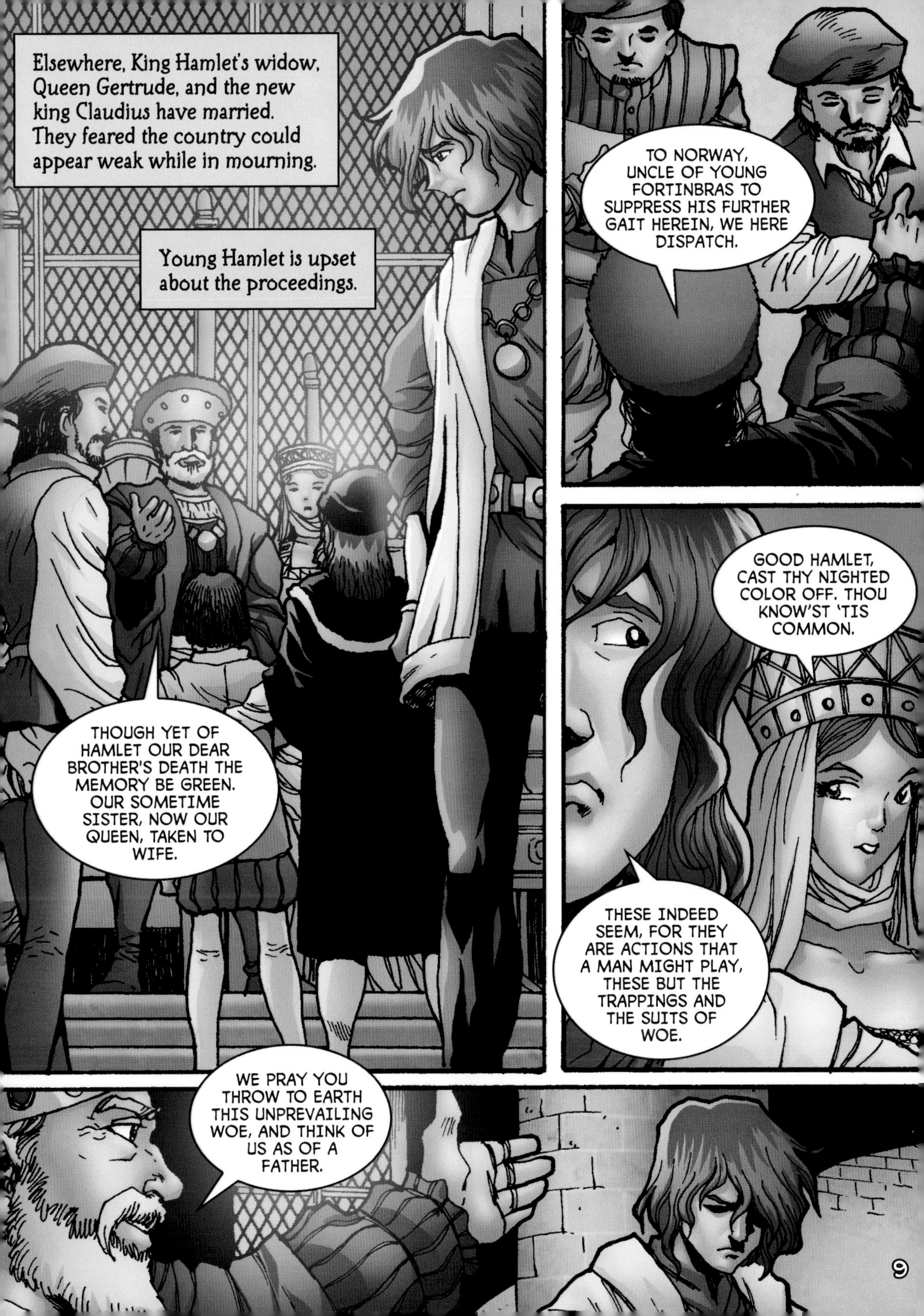
Elsewhere, King Hamlet's widow, Queen Gertrude, and the new king Claudius have married. They feared the country could appear weak while in mourning.
Young Hamlet is upset about the proceedings.
THOUGH YET OF HAMLET OUR DEAR BROTHER'S DEATH THE MEMORY BE GREEN. OUR SOMETIME SISTER, NOW OUR QUEEN, TAKEN TO WIFE.
TO NORWAY, UNCLE OF YOUNG FORTINBRAS TO SUPPRESS HIS FURTHER GAIT HEREIN, WE HERE DISPATCH.
GOOD HAMLET, CAST THY NIGHTED COLOR OFF. THOU KNOW'ST 'TIS COMMON.
THESE INDEED SEEM, FOR THEY ARE ACTIONS THAT A MAN MIGHT PLAY, THESE BUT THE TRAPPINGS AND THE SUITS OF WOE.
WE PRAY YOU THROW TO EARTH THIS UNPREVAILING WOE, AND THINK OF US AS OF A FATHER.

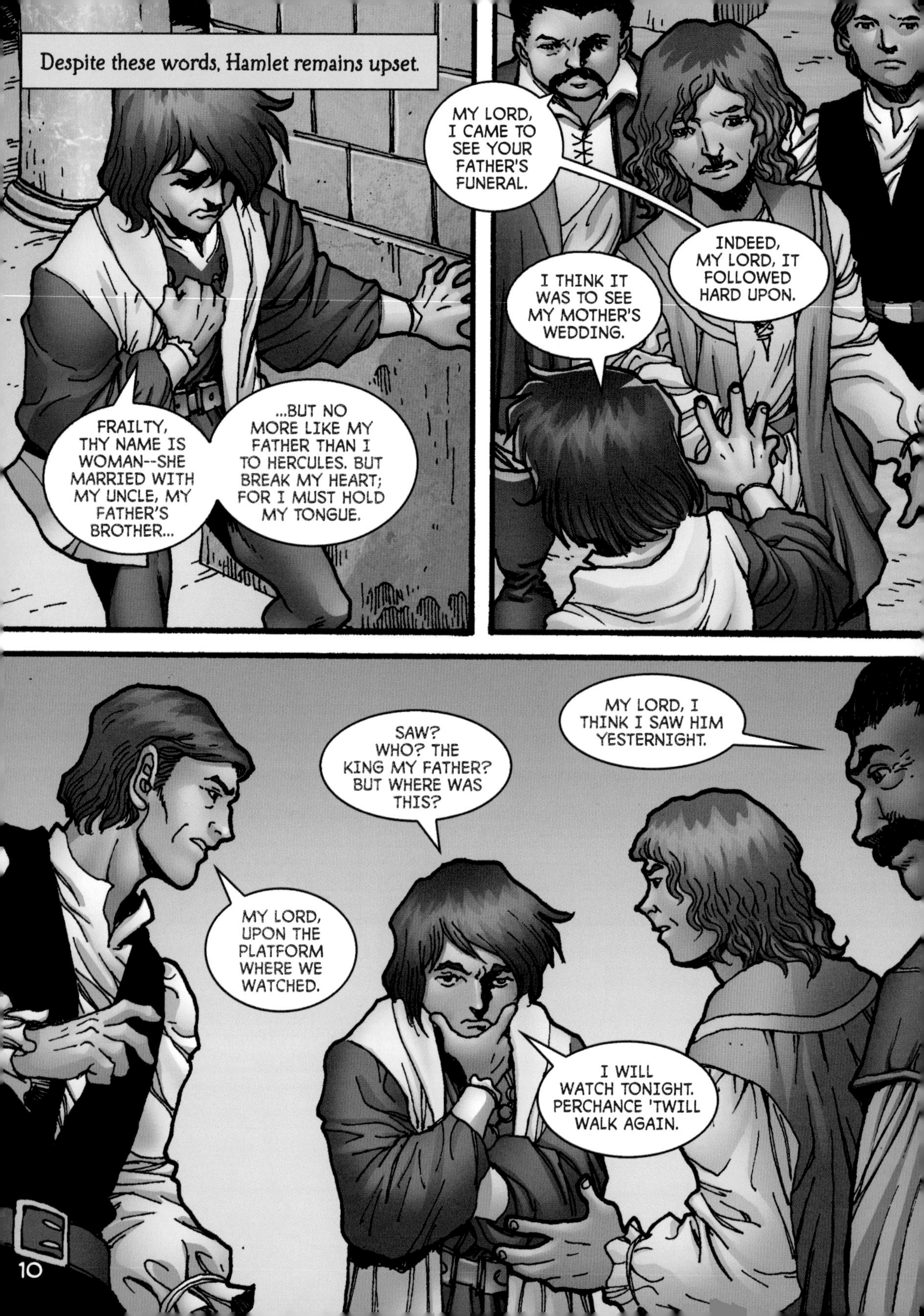
Despite these words, Hamlet remains upset.
FRAILTY, THY NAME IS WOMAN--SHE MARRIED WITH MY UNCLE, MY FATHER'S BROTHER...
...BUT NO MORE LIKE MY FATHER THAN I TO HERCULES. BUT BREAK MY HEART; FOR I MUST HOLD MY TONGUE.
MY LORD, I CAME TO SEE YOUR FATHER'S FUNERAL.
I THINK IT WAS TO SEE MY MOTHER'S WEDDING.
INDEED, MY LORD, IT FOLLOWED HARD UPON.
MY LORD, I THINK I SAW HIM YESTERNIGHT.
SAW? WHO? THE KING MY FATHER? BUT WHERE WAS THIS?
MY LORD, UPON THE PLATFORM WHERE WE WATCHED.
I WILL WATCH TONIGHT. PERCHANCE 'TWILL WALK AGAIN.

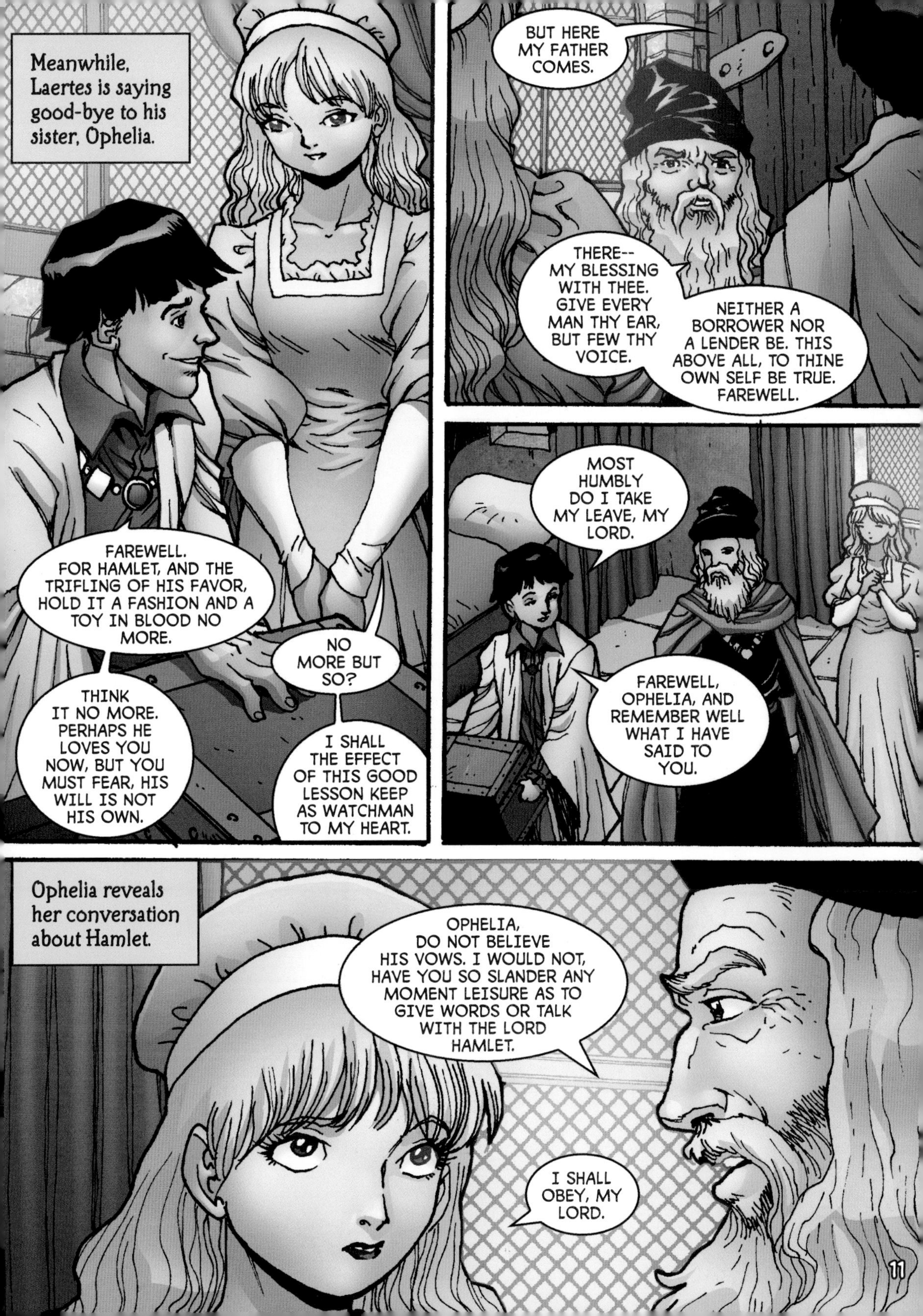

Meanwhile, Laertes is saying good-bye to his sister, Ophelia.
FAREWELL. FOR HAMLET, AND THE TRIFLING OF HIS FAVOR, HOLD IT A FASHION AND A TOY IN BLOOD NO MORE.
NO MORE BUT SO?
THINK IT NO MORE. PERHAPS HE LOVES YOU NOW, BUT YOU MUST FEAR, HIS WILL IS NOT HIS OWN.
I SHALL THE EFFECT OF THIS GOOD LESSON KEEP AS WATCHMAN TO MY HEART.
BUT HERE MY FATHER COMES.
THERE-- MY BLESSING WITH THEE. GIVE EVERY MAN THY EAR, BUT FEW THY VOICE.
NEITHER A BORROWER NOR A LENDER BE. THIS ABOVE ALL, TO THINE OWN SELF BE TRUE. FAREWELL.
MOST HUMBLY DO I TAKE MY LEAVE, MY LORD.
FAREWELL, OPHELIA, AND REMEMBER WELL WHAT I HAVE SAID TO YOU.
Ophelia reveals her conversation about Hamlet.
OPHELIA, DO NOT BELIEVE HIS VOWS. I WOULD NOT, HAVE YOU SO SLANDER ANY MOMENT LEISURE AS TO GIVE WORDS OR TALK WITH THE LORD HAMLET.
I SHALL OBEY, MY LORD.

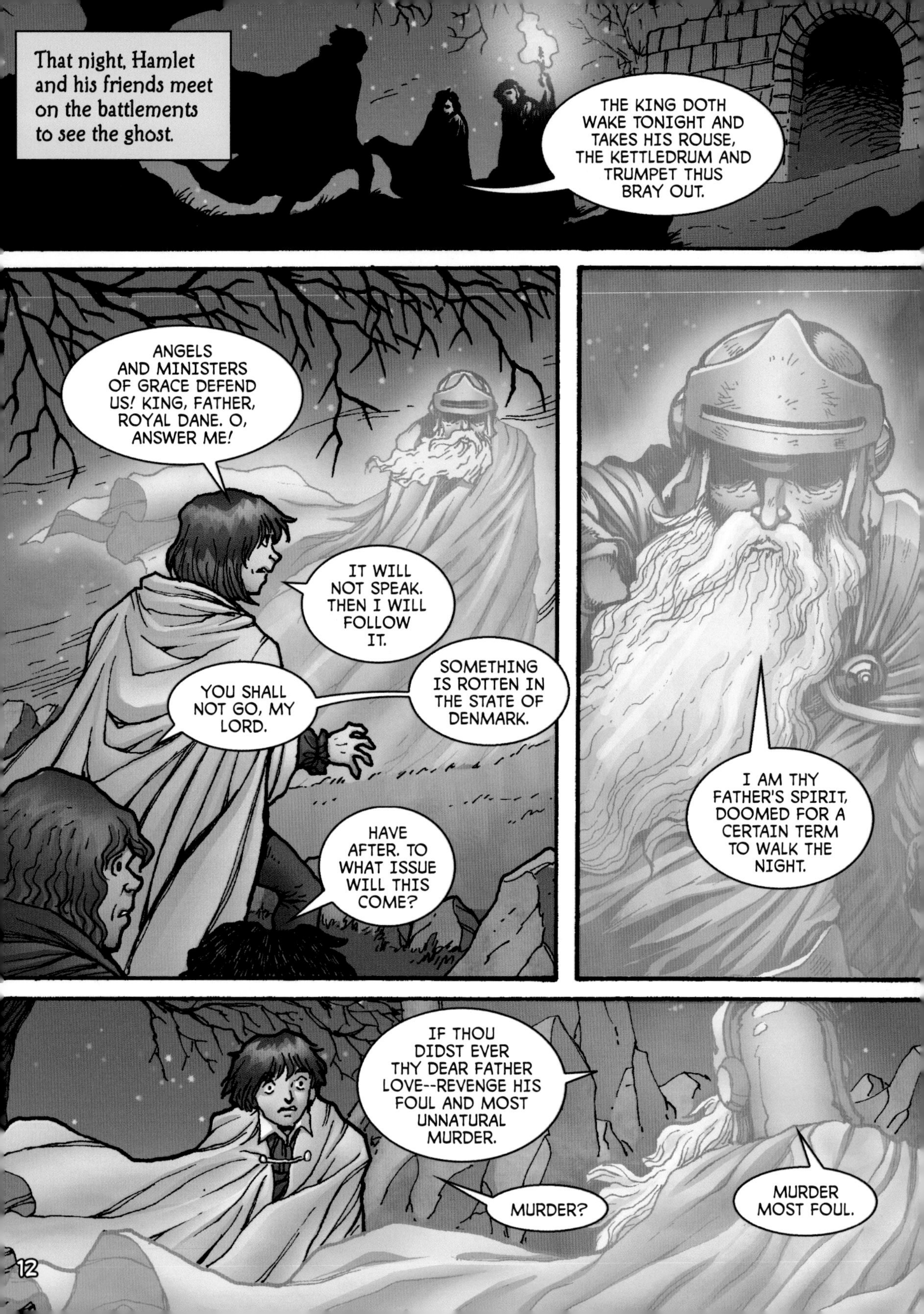

That night, Hamlet and his friends meet on the battlements to see the ghost.
THE KING DOTH WAKE TONIGHT AND TAKES HIS ROUSE, THE KETTLEDRUM AND TRUMPET THUS BRAY OUT.
ANGELS AND MINISTERS OF GRACE DEFEND US! KING, FATHER, ROYAL DANE. O, ANSWER ME!
IT WILL NOT SPEAK. THEN I WILL FOLLOW IT.
YOU SHALL NOT GO, MY LORD.
SOMETHING IS ROTTEN IN THE STATE OF DENMARK.
HAVE AFTER. TO WHAT ISSUE WILL THIS COME?
I AM THY FATHER'S SPIRIT, DOOMED FOR A CERTAIN TERM TO WALK THE NIGHT.
IF THOU DIDST EVER THY DEAR FATHER LOVE--REVENGE HIS FOUL AND MOST UNNATURAL MURDER.
MURDER?
MURDER MOST FOUL.

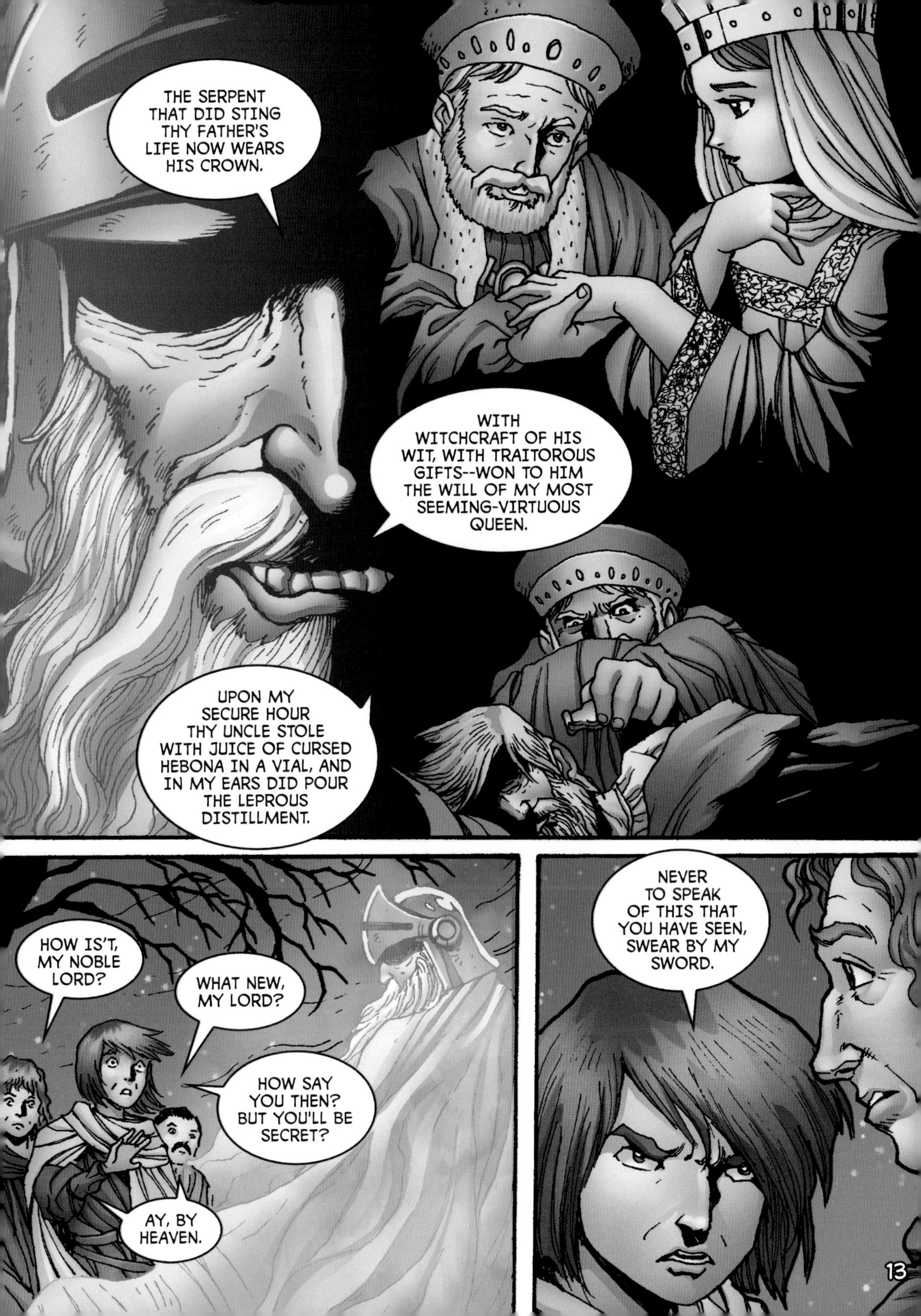
THE SERPENT THAT DID STING THY FATHER'S LIFE NOW WEARS HIS CROWN.
WITH WITCHCRAFT OF HIS WIT, WITH TRAITOROUS GIFTS--WON TO HIM THE WILL OF MY MOST SEEMING-VIRTUOUS QUEEN.
UPON MY SECURE HOUR THY UNCLE STOLE WITH JUICE OF CURSED HEBONA IN A VIAL, AND IN MY EARS DID POUR THE LEPROUS DISTILLMENT.
HOW IS'T, MY NOBLE LORD?
WHAT NEW, MY LORD?
HOW SAY YOU THEN? BUT YOU'LL BE SECRET?
AY, BY HEAVEN.
NEVER TO SPEAK OF THIS THAT YOU HAVE SEEN, SWEAR BY MY SWORD.

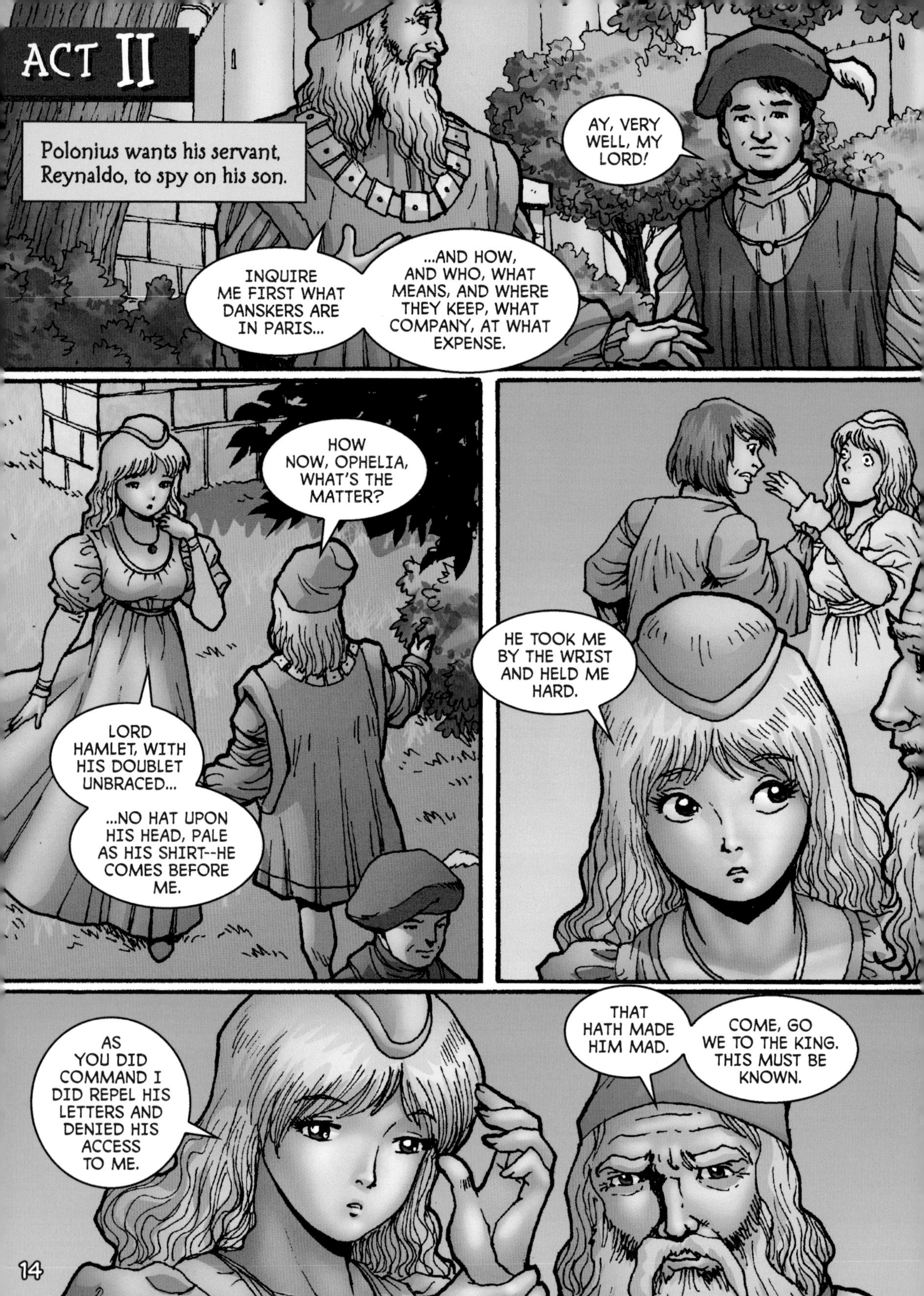
ACT II
Polonius wants his servant, Reynaldo, to spy on his son.
AY, VERY WELL, MY LORD!
INQUIRE ME FIRST WHAT DANSKERS ARE IN PARIS...
...AND HOW, AND WHO, WHAT MEANS, AND WHERE THEY KEEP, WHAT COMPANY, AT WHAT EXPENSE.
HOW NOW, OPHELIA, WHAT'S THE MATTER?
LORD HAMLET, WITH HIS DOUBLET UNBRACED...
...NO HAT UPON HIS HEAD, PALE AS HIS SHIRT--HE COMES BEFORE ME.
HE TOOK ME BY THE WRIST AND HELD ME HARD.
AS YOU DID COMMAND I DID REPEL HIS LETTERS AND DENIED HIS ACCESS TO ME.
THAT HATH MADE HIM MAD.
COME, GO WE TO THE KING. THIS MUST BE KNOWN.

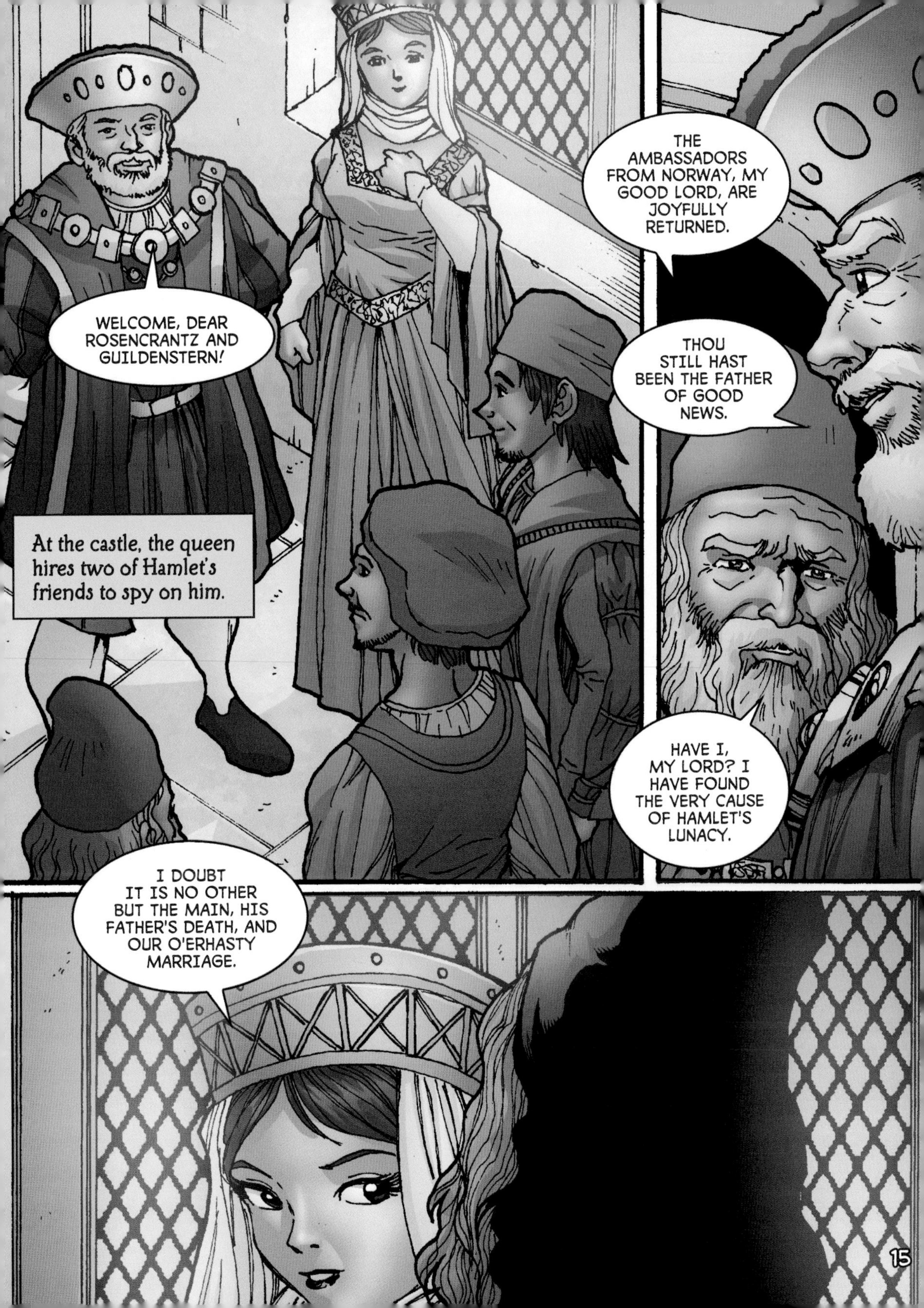
WELCOME, DEAR ROSENCRANTZ AND GUILDENSTERN!
At the castle, the queen hires two of Hamlet's friends to spy on him.
THE AMBASSADORS FROM NORWAY, MY GOOD LORD, ARE JOYFULLY RETURNED.
THOU STILL HAST BEEN THE FATHER OF GOOD NEWS.
HAVE I, MY LORD? I HAVE FOUND THE VERY CAUSE OF HAMLET'S LUNACY.
I DOUBT IT IS NO OTHER BUT THE MAIN, HIS FATHER'S DEATH, AND OUR O'ERHASTY MARRIAGE.

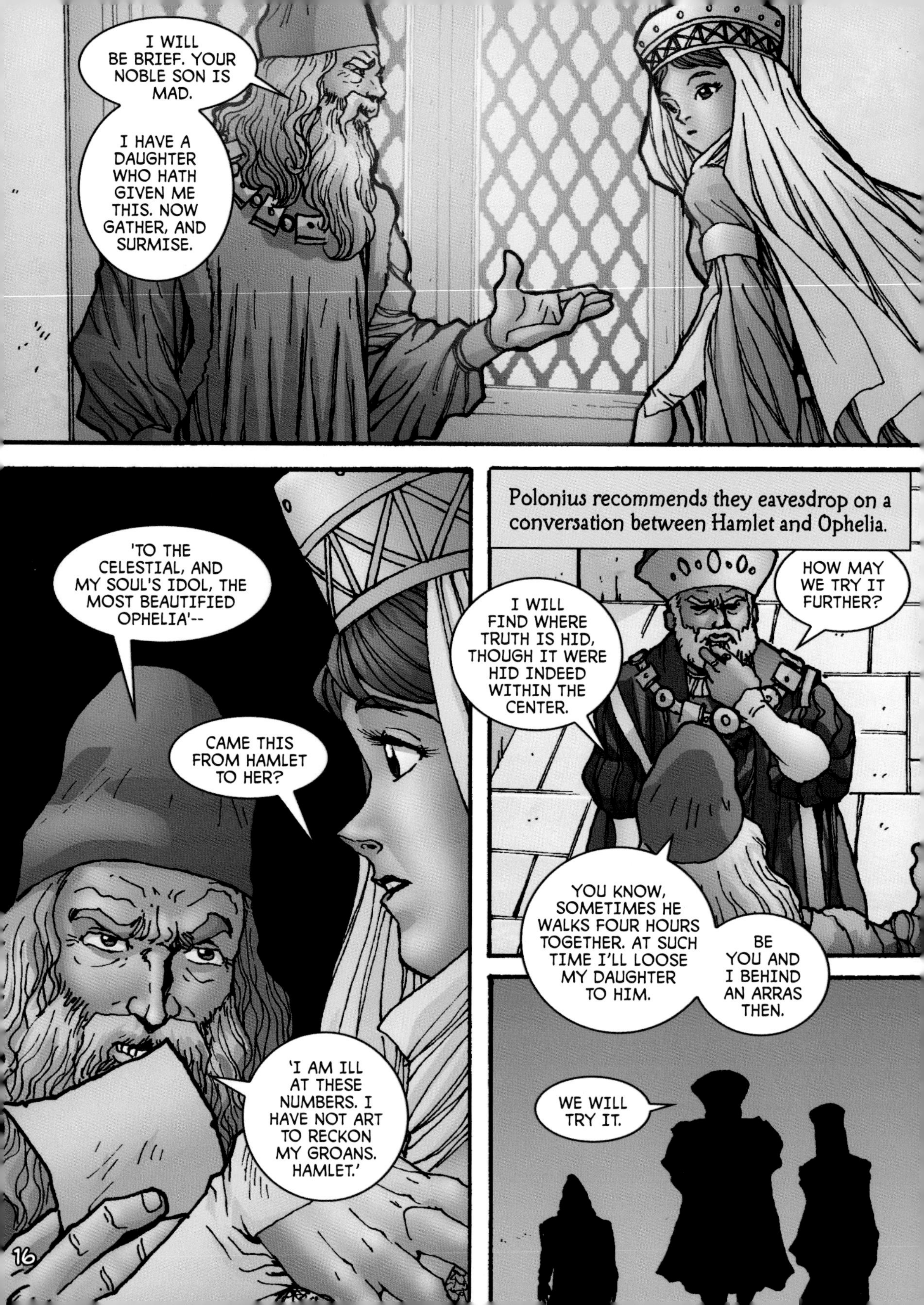
I WILL BE BRIEF. YOUR NOBLE SON IS MAD.
I HAVE A DAUGHTER WHO HATH GIVEN ME THIS. NOW GATHER, AND SURMISE.
'TO THE CELESTIAL, AND MY SOUL'S IDOL, THE MOST BEAUTIFIED OPHELIA'--
CAME THIS FROM HAMLET TO HER?
'I AM ILL AT THESE NUMBERS. I HAVE NOT ART TO RECKON MY GROANS. HAMLET.'
Polonius recommends they eavesdrop on a conversation between Hamlet and Ophelia.
I WILL FIND WHERE TRUTH IS HID, THOUGH IT WERE HID INDEED WITHIN THE CENTER.
HOW MAY WE TRY IT FURTHER?
YOU KNOW, SOMETIMES HE WALKS FOUR HOURS TOGETHER. AT SUCH TIME I'LL LOOSE MY DAUGHTER TO HIM.
BE YOU AND I BEHIND AN ARRAS THEN.
WE WILL TRY IT.

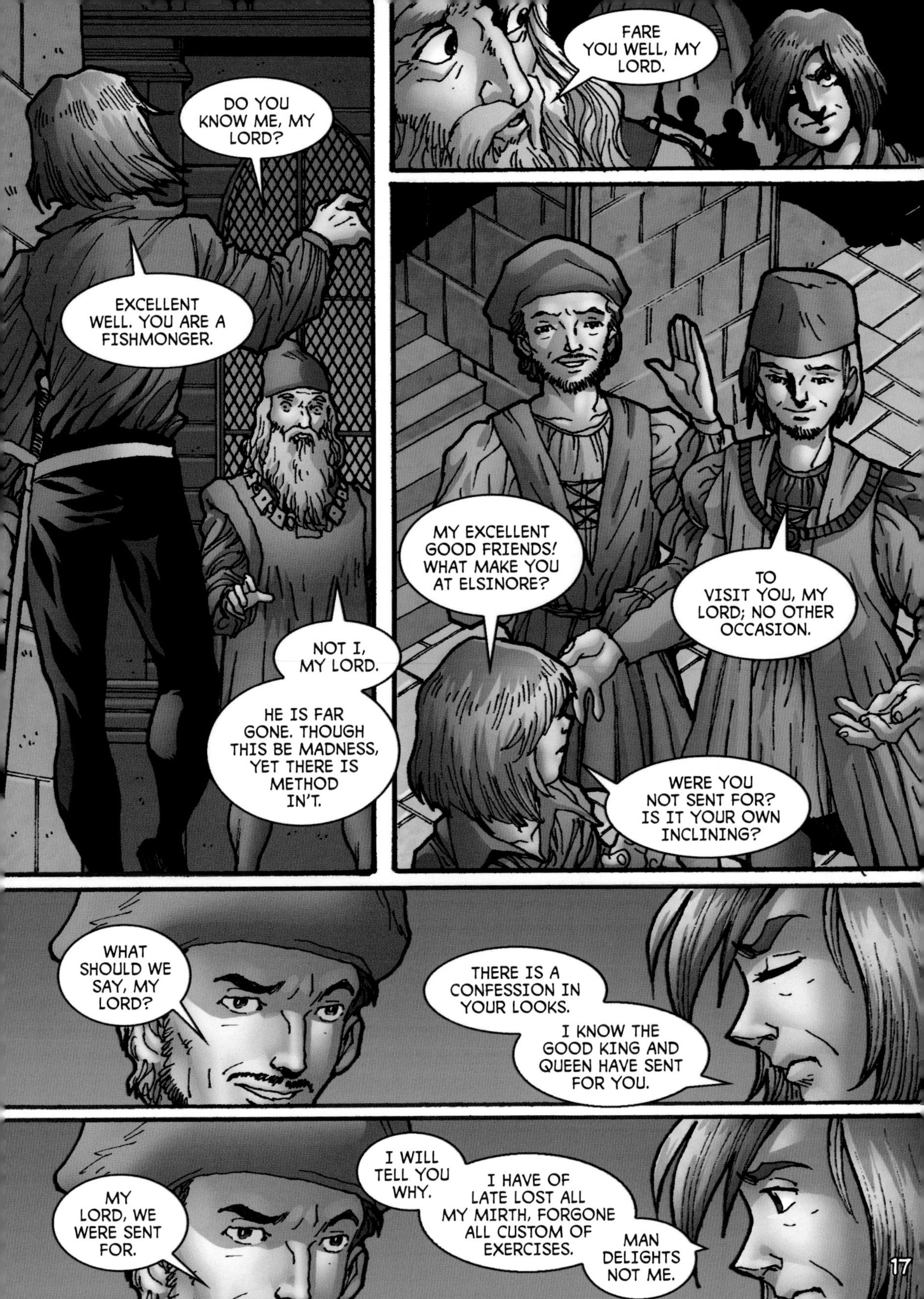
DO YOU KNOW ME, MY LORD?
EXCELLENT WELL. YOU ARE A FISHMONGER.
NOT I, MY LORD.
HE IS FAR GONE. THOUGH THIS BE MADNESS, YET THERE IS METHOD IN'T.
FARE YOU WELL, MY LORD.
MY EXCELLENT GOOD FRIENDS! WHAT MAKE YOU AT ELSINORE?
TO VISIT YOU, MY LORD; NO OTHER OCCASION.
WERE YOU NOT SENT FOR? IS IT YOUR OWN INCLINING?
WHAT SHOULD WE SAY, MY LORD?
THERE IS A CONFESSION IN YOUR LOOKS.
I KNOW THE GOOD KING AND QUEEN HAVE SENT FOR YOU.
MY LORD, WE WERE SENT FOR.
I WILL TELL YOU WHY.
I HAVE OF LATE LOST ALL MY MIRTH, FORGONE ALL CUSTOM OF EXERCISES.
MAN DELIGHTS NOT ME.

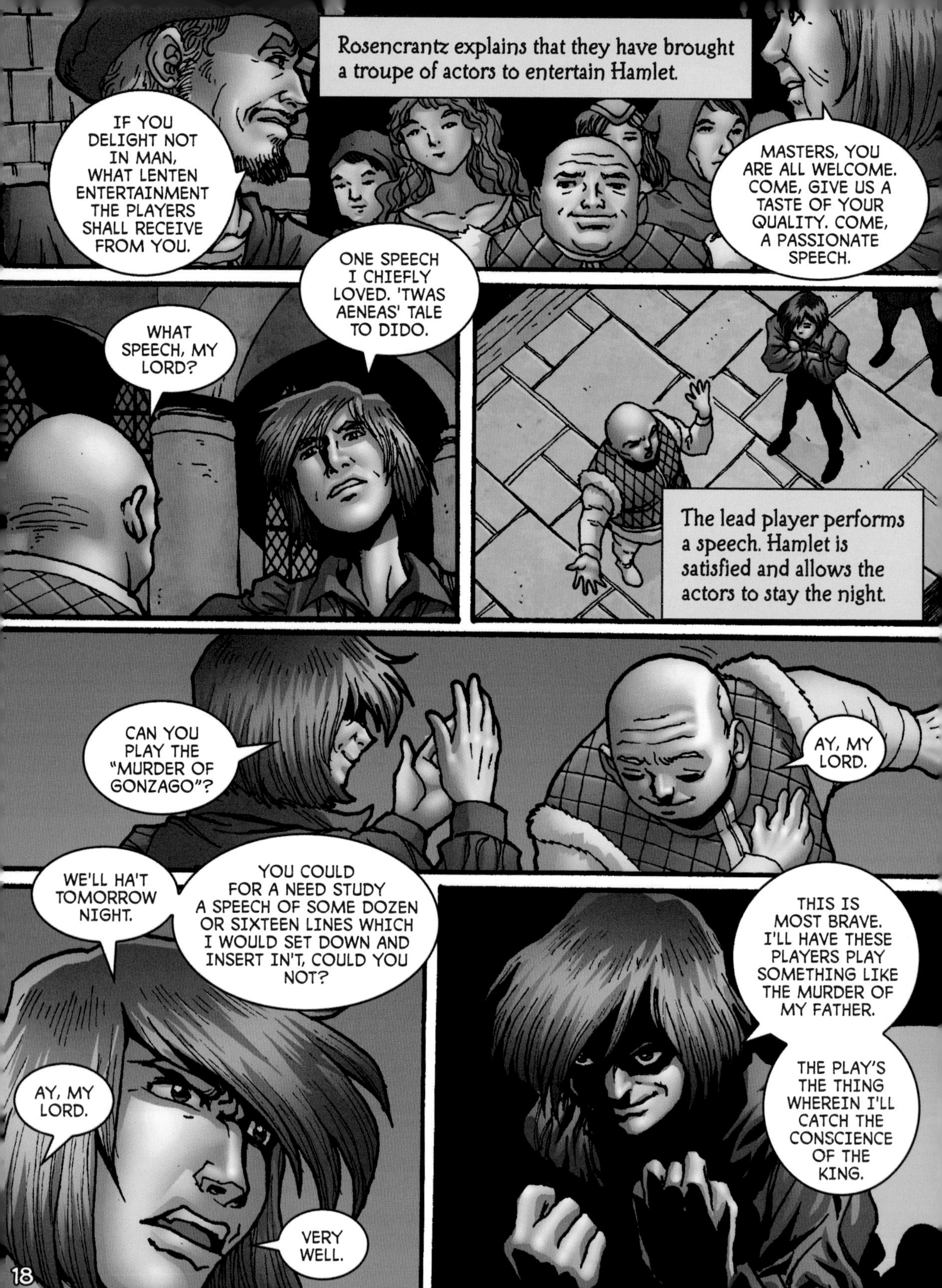

Rosencrantz explains that they have brought a troupe of actors to entertain Hamlet.
IF YOU DELIGHT NOT IN MAN, WHAT LENTEN ENTERTAINMENT THE PLAYERS SHALL RECEIVE FROM YOU.
MASTERS, YOU ARE ALL WELCOME. COME, GIVE US A TASTE OF YOUR QUALITY. COME, A PASSIONATE SPEECH.
WHAT SPEECH, MY LORD?
ONE SPEECH I CHIEFLY LOVED. 'TWAS AENEAS' TALE TO DIDO.
The lead player performs a speech. Hamlet is satisfied and allows the actors to stay the night.
CAN YOU PLAY THE "MURDER OF GONZAGO"?
AY, MY LORD.
WE'LL HA'T TOMORROW NIGHT.
YOU COULD FOR A NEED STUDY A SPEECH OF SOME DOZEN OR SIXTEEN LINES WHICH I WOULD SET DOWN AND INSERT IN'T, COULD YOU NOT?
AY, MY LORD.
VERY WELL.
THIS IS MOST BRAVE. I'LL HAVE THESE PLAYERS PLAY SOMETHING LIKE THE MURDER OF MY FATHER.
THE PLAY'S THE THING WHEREIN I'LL CATCH THE CONSCIENCE OF THE KING.

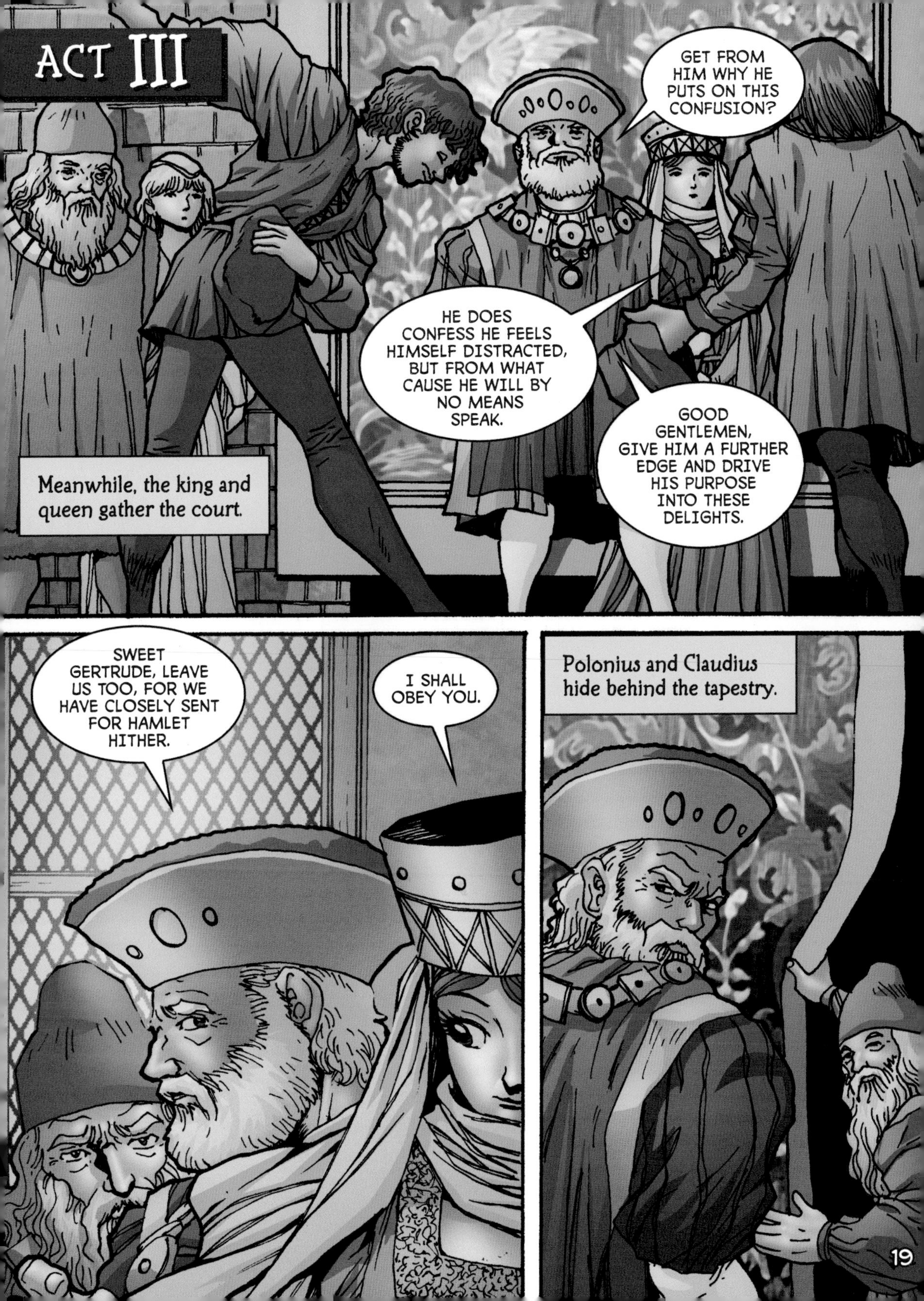
ACT III
Meanwhile, the king and queen gather the court.
GET FROM HIM WHY HE PUTS ON THIS CONFUSION?
HE DOES CONFESS HE FEELS HIMSELF DISTRACTED, BUT FROM WHAT CAUSE HE WILL BY NO MEANS SPEAK.
GOOD GENTLEMEN, GIVE HIM A FURTHER EDGE AND DRIVE HIS PURPOSE INTO THESE DELIGHTS.
SWEET GERTRUDE, LEAVE US TOO, FOR WE HAVE CLOSELY SENT FOR HAMLET HITHER.
I SHALL OBEY YOU.
Polonius and Claudius hide behind the tapestry.

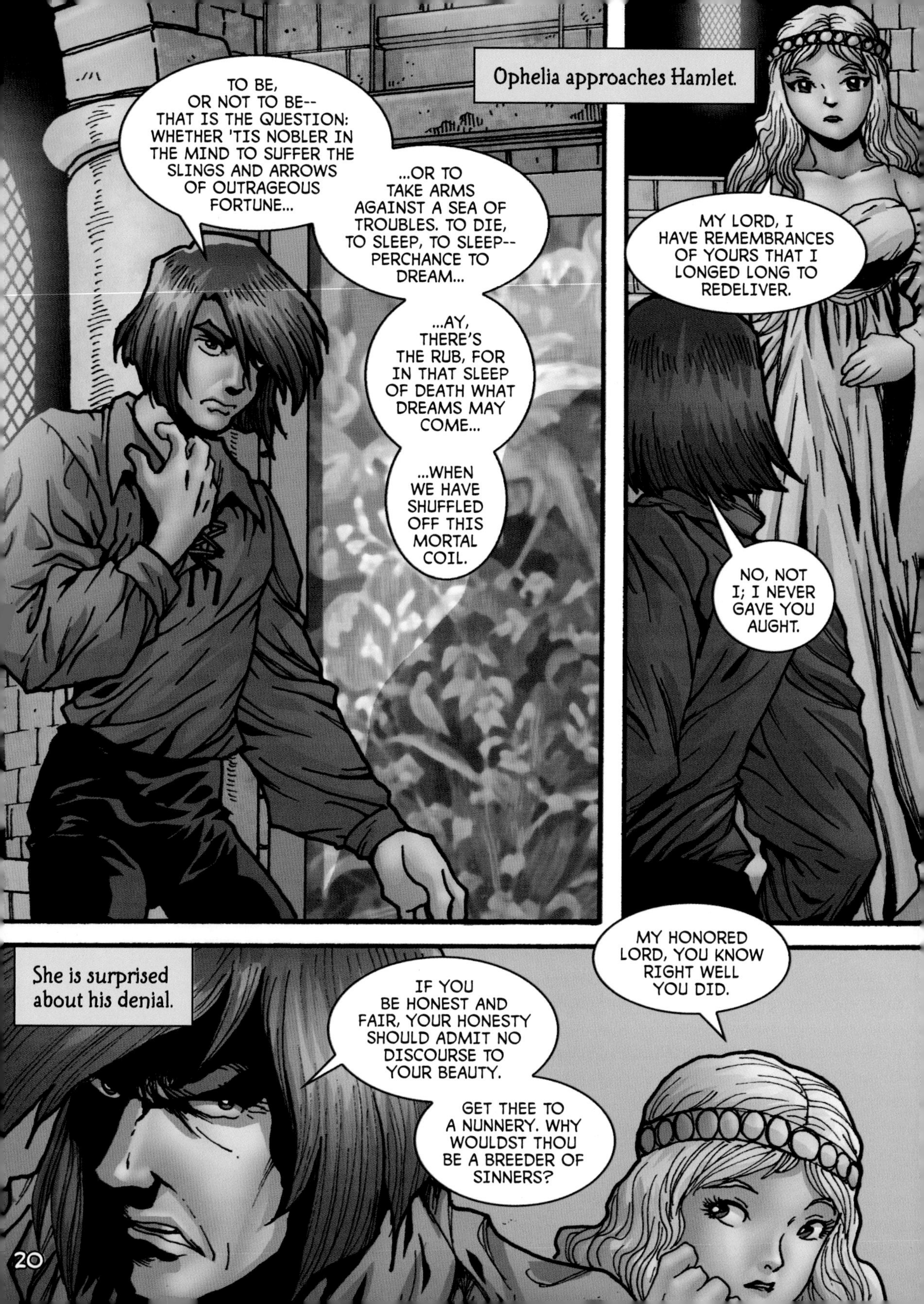

TO BE, OR NOT TO BE-- THAT IS THE QUESTION: WHETHER 'TIS NOBLER IN THE MIND TO SUFFER THE SLINGS AND ARROWS OF OUTRAGEOUS FORTUNE...
...OR TO TAKE ARMS AGAINST A SEA OF TROUBLES. TO DIE, TO SLEEP, TO SLEEP-- PERCHANCE TO DREAM...
...AY, THERE'S THE RUB, FOR IN THAT SLEEP OF DEATH WHAT DREAMS MAY COME...
...WHEN WE HAVE SHUFFLED OFF THIS MORTAL COIL.
Ophelia approaches Hamlet.
MY LORD, I HAVE REMEMBRANCES OF YOURS THAT I LONGED LONG TO REDELIVER.
NO, NOT I; I NEVER GAVE YOU AUGHT.
She is surprised about his denial.
MY HONORED LORD, YOU KNOW RIGHT WELL YOU DID.
IF YOU BE HONEST AND FAIR, YOUR HONESTY SHOULD ADMIT NO DISCOURSE TO YOUR BEAUTY.
GET THEE TO A NUNNERY. WHY WOULDST THOU BE A BREEDER OF SINNERS?

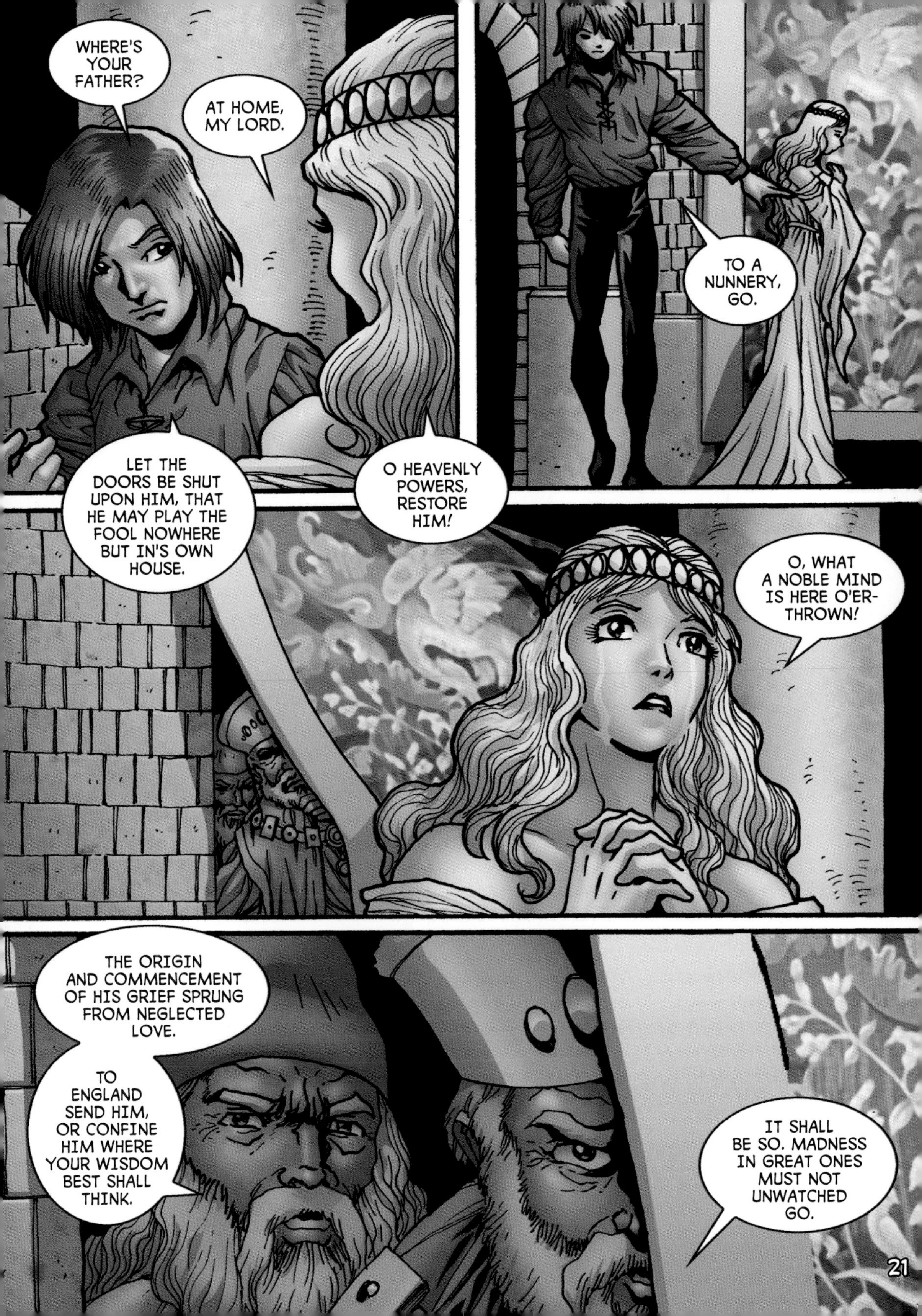
WHERE'S YOUR FATHER?
AT HOME, MY LORD.
LET THE DOORS BE SHUT UPON HIM, THAT HE MAY PLAY THE FOOL NOWHERE BUT IN'S OWN HOUSE.
O HEAVENLY POWERS, RESTORE HIM!
TO A NUNNERY, GO.
O, WHAT A NOBLE MIND IS HERE O'ER-THROWN!
THE ORIGIN AND COMMENCEMENT OF HIS GRIEF SPRUNG FROM NEGLECTED LOVE.
TO ENGLAND SEND HIM, OR CONFINE HIM WHERE YOUR WISDOM BEST SHALL THINK.
IT SHALL BE SO. MADNESS IN GREAT ONES MUST NOT UNWATCHED GO.

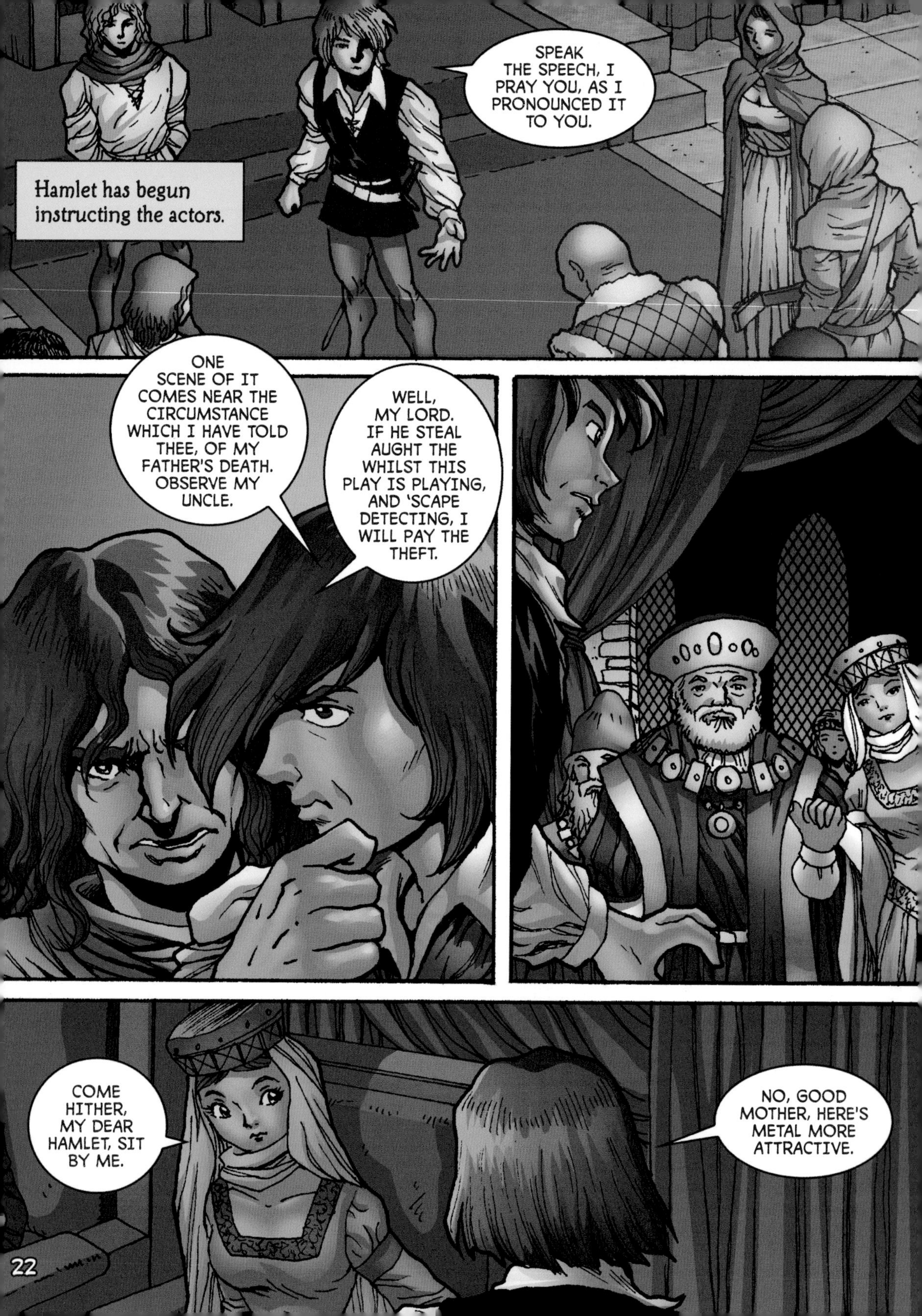
Hamlet has begun instructing the actors.
SPEAK THE SPEECH, I PRAY YOU, AS I PRONOUNCED IT TO YOU.
ONE SCENE OF IT COMES NEAR THE CIRCUMSTANCE WHICH I HAVE TOLD THEE, OF MY FATHER'S DEATH. OBSERVE MY UNCLE.
WELL, MY LORD. IF HE STEAL AUGHT THE WHILST THIS PLAY IS PLAYING, AND 'SCAPE DETECTING, I WILL PAY THE THEFT.
COME HITHER, MY DEAR HAMLET, SIT BY ME.
NO, GOOD MOTHER, HERE'S METAL MORE ATTRACTIVE.

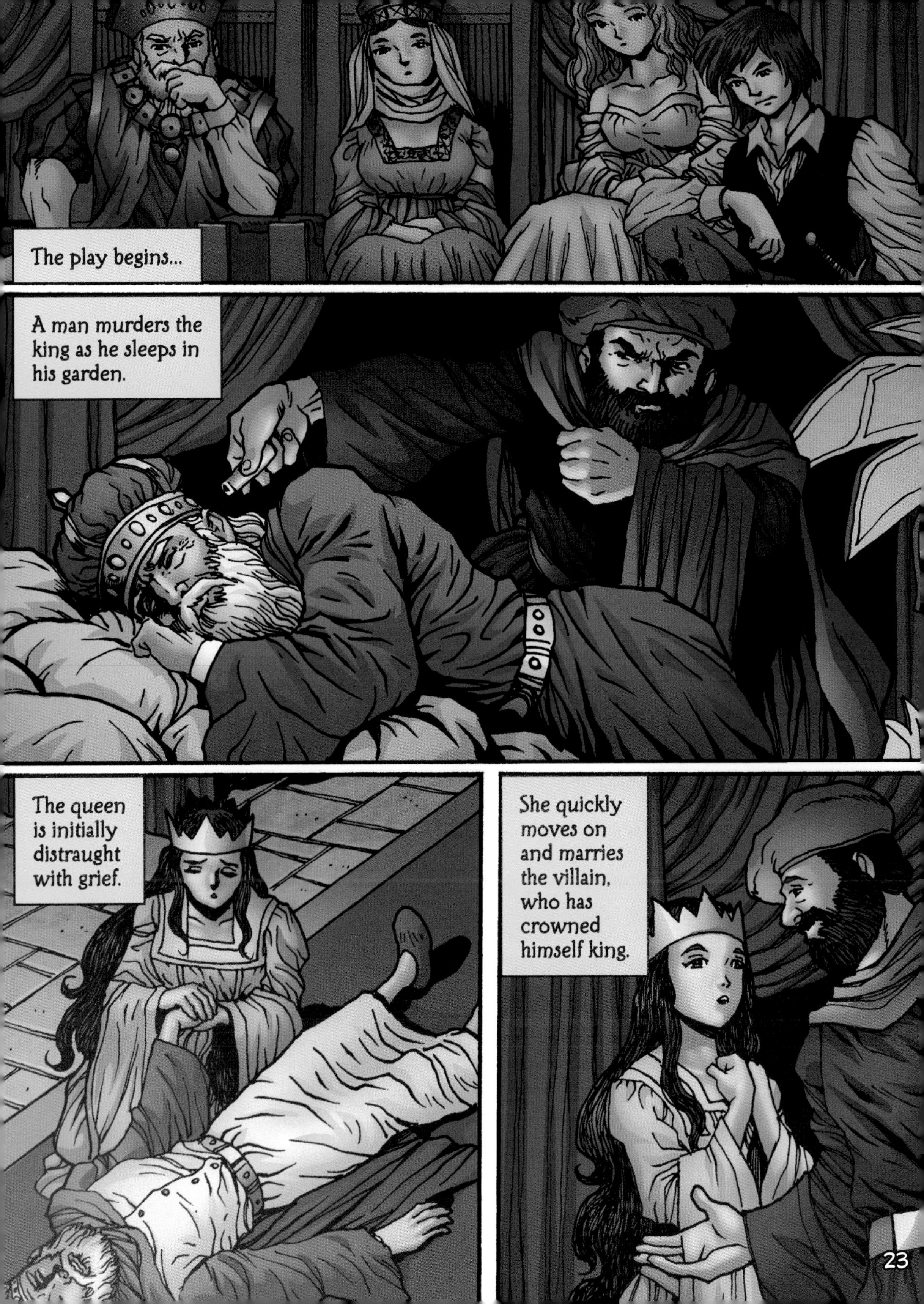
The play begins...
A man murders the king as he sleeps in his garden.
The queen is initially distraught with grief.
She quickly moves on and marries the villain, who has crowned himself king.

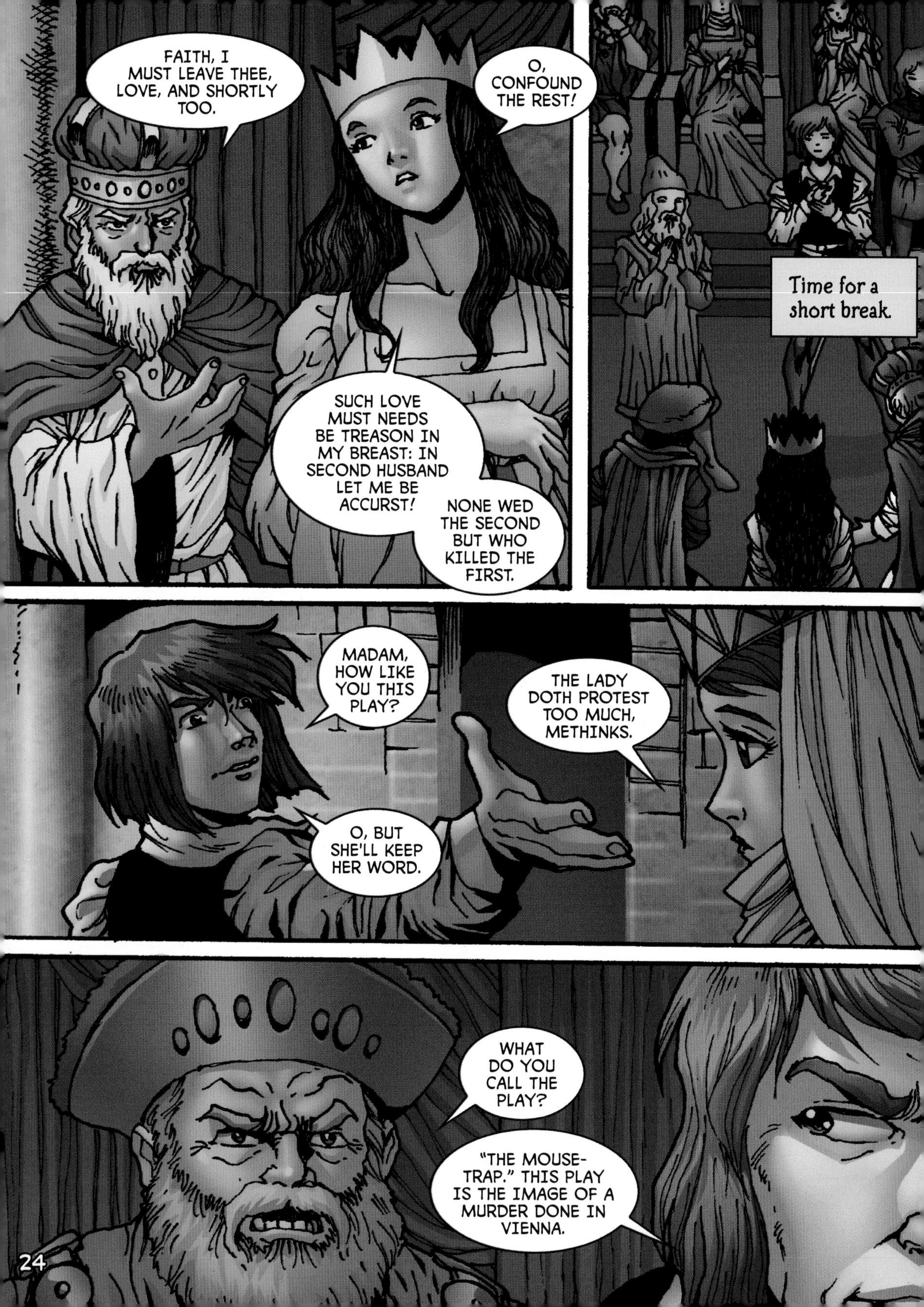
FAITH, I MUST LEAVE THEE, LOVE, AND SHORTLY TOO.
O, CONFOUND THE REST!
SUCH LOVE MUST NEEDS BE TREASON IN MY BREAST: IN SECOND HUSBAND LET ME BE ACCURST!
NONE WED THE SECOND BUT WHO KILLED THE FIRST.
Time for a short break.
MADAM, HOW LIKE YOU THIS PLAY?
THE LADY DOTH PROTEST TOO MUCH, METHINKS.
O, BUT SHE'LL KEEP HER WORD.
WHAT DO YOU CALL THE PLAY?
"THE MOUSE-TRAP." THIS PLAY IS THE IMAGE OF A MURDER DONE IN VIENNA.

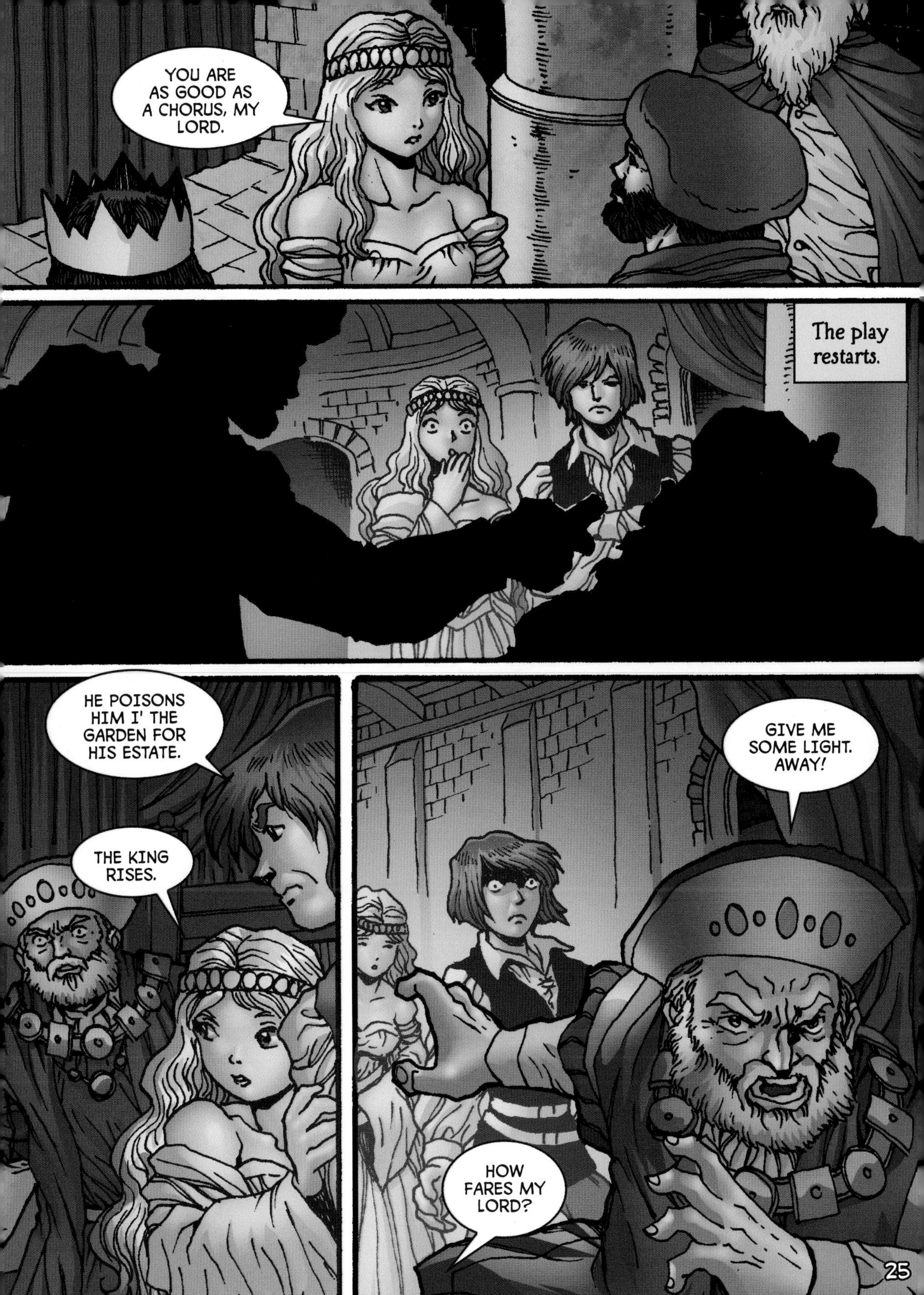
YOU ARE AS GOOD AS A CHORUS, MY LORD.
The play restarts.
HE POISONS HIM I' THE GARDEN FOR HIS ESTATE.
THE KING RISES.
GIVE ME SOME LIGHT. AWAY!
HOW FARES MY LORD?

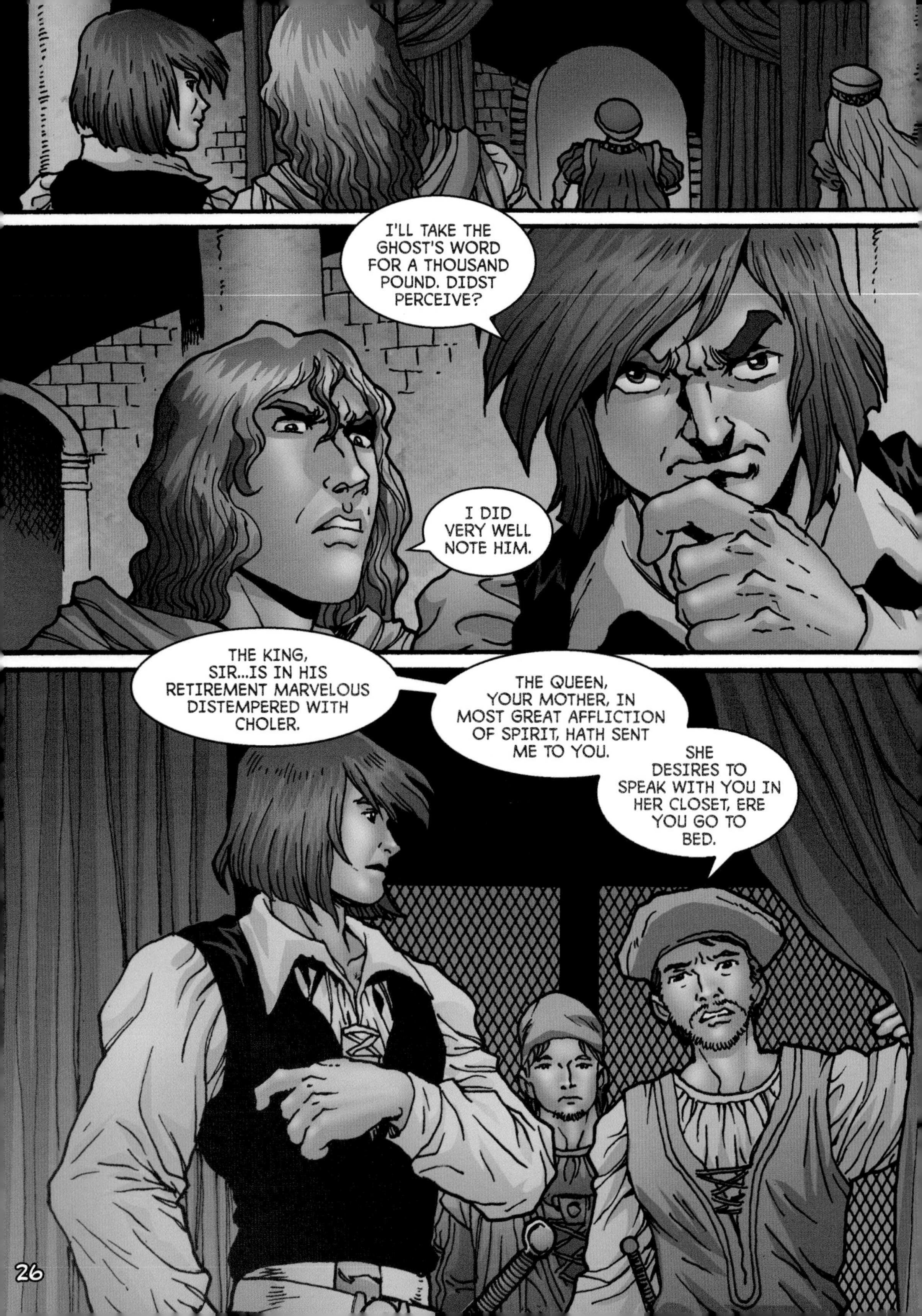
I'LL TAKE THE GHOST'S WORD FOR A THOUSAND POUND. DIDST PERCEIVE?
I DID VERY WELL NOTE HIM.
THE KING, SIR...IS IN HIS RETIREMENT MARVELOUS DISTEMPERED WITH CHOLER.
THE QUEEN, YOUR MOTHER, IN MOST GREAT AFFLICTION OF SPIRIT, HATH SENT ME TO YOU.
SHE DESIRES TO SPEAK WITH YOU IN HER CLOSET, ERE YOU GO TO BED.

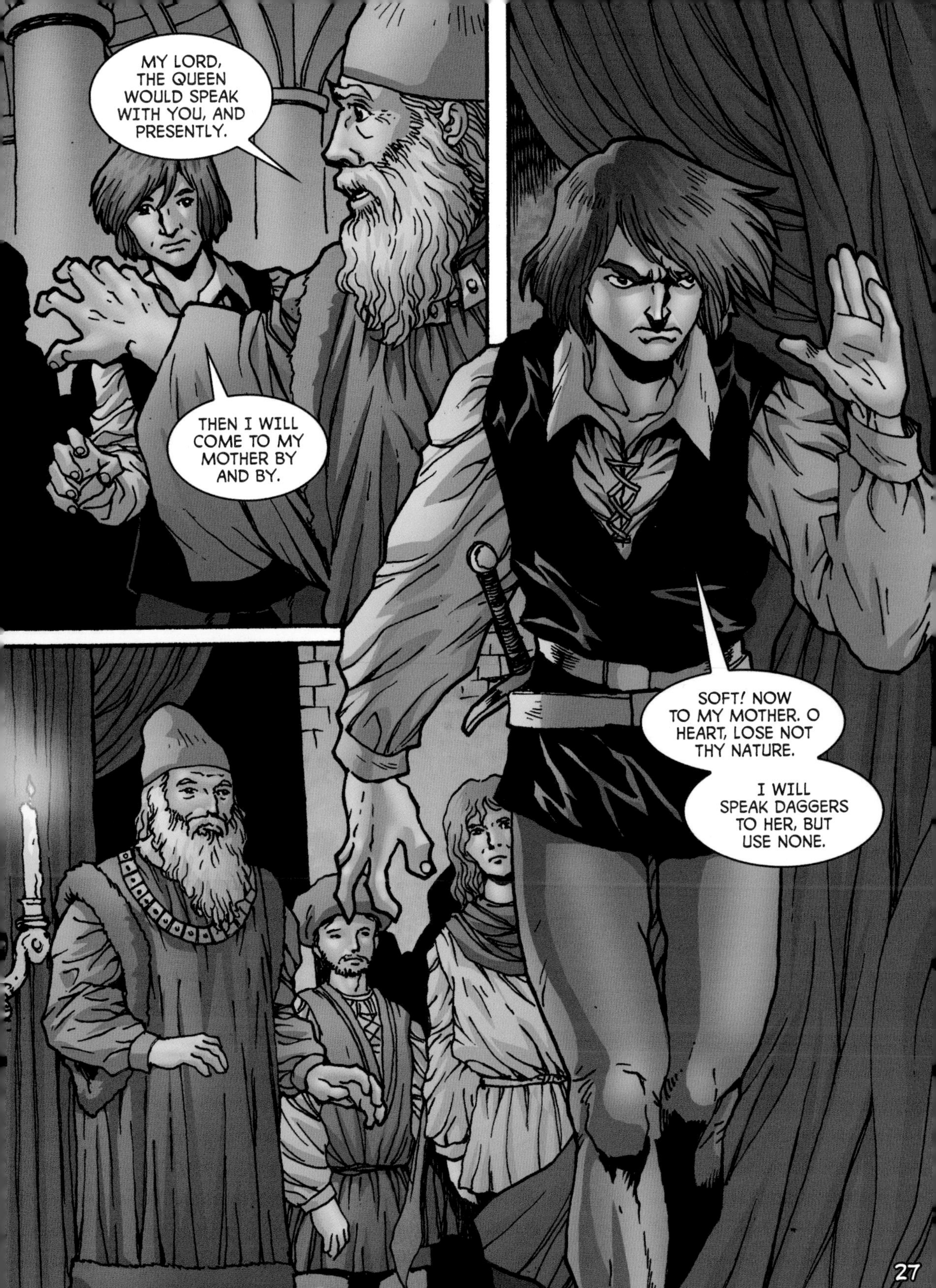
MY LORD, THE QUEEN WOULD SPEAK WITH YOU, AND PRESENTLY.
THEN I WILL COME TO MY MOTHER BY AND BY.
SOFT! NOW TO MY MOTHER. O HEART, LOSE NOT THY NATURE.
I WILL SPEAK DAGGERS TO HER, BUT USE NONE.

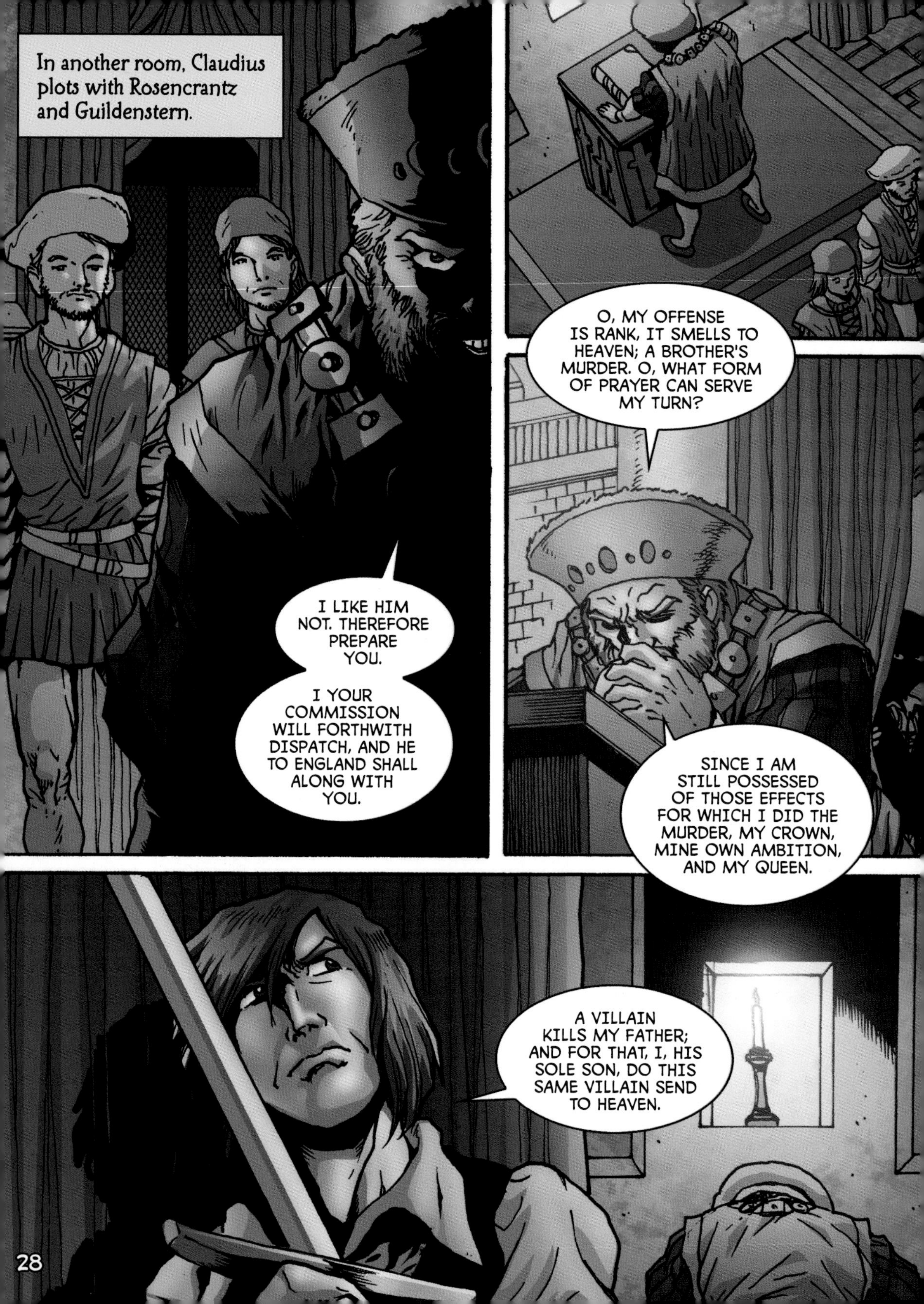
In another room, Claudius plots with Rosencrantz and Guildenstern.
I LIKE HIM NOT. THEREFORE PREPARE YOU.
I YOUR COMMISSION WILL FORTHWITH DISPATCH, AND HE TO ENGLAND SHALL ALONG WITH YOU.
O, MY OFFENSE IS RANK, IT SMELLS TO HEAVEN; A BROTHER'S MURDER. O, WHAT FORM OF PRAYER CAN SERVE MY TURN?
SINCE I AM STILL POSSESSED OF THOSE EFFECTS FOR WHICH I DID THE MURDER, MY CROWN, MINE OWN AMBITION, AND MY QUEEN.
A VILLAIN KILLS MY FATHER; AND FOR THAT, I, HIS SOLE SON, DO THIS SAME VILLAIN SEND TO HEAVEN.

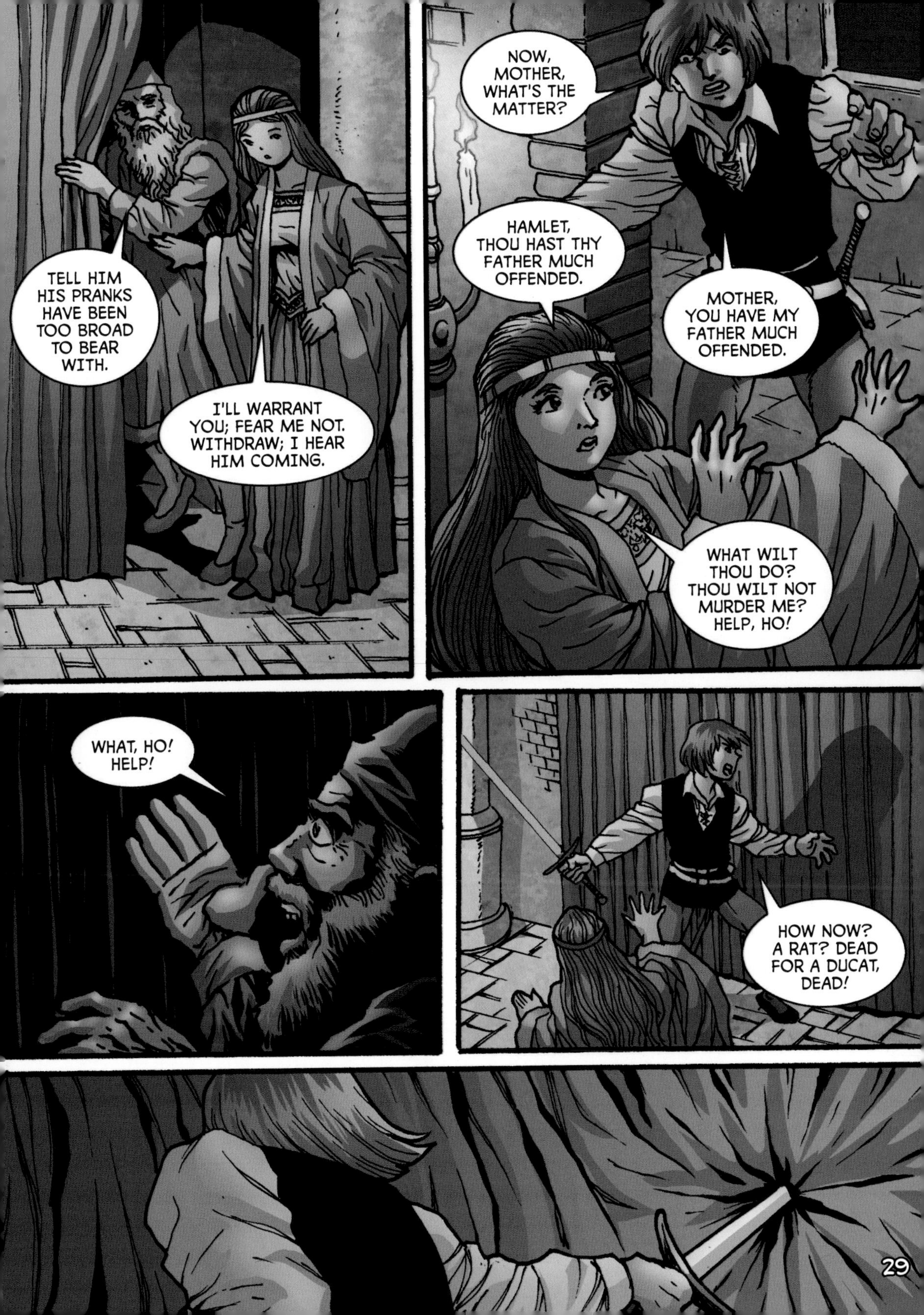
TELL HIM HIS PRANKS HAVE BEEN TOO BROAD TO BEAR WITH.
I'LL WARRANT YOU; FEAR ME NOT. WITHDRAW; I HEAR HIM COMING.
NOW, MOTHER, WHAT'S THE MATTER?
HAMLET, THOU HAST THY FATHER MUCH OFFENDED.
MOTHER, YOU HAVE MY FATHER MUCH OFFENDED.
WHAT WILT THOU DO? THOU WILT NOT MURDER ME? HELP, HO!
WHAT, HO! HELP!
HOW NOW? A RAT? DEAD FOR A DUCAT, DEAD!

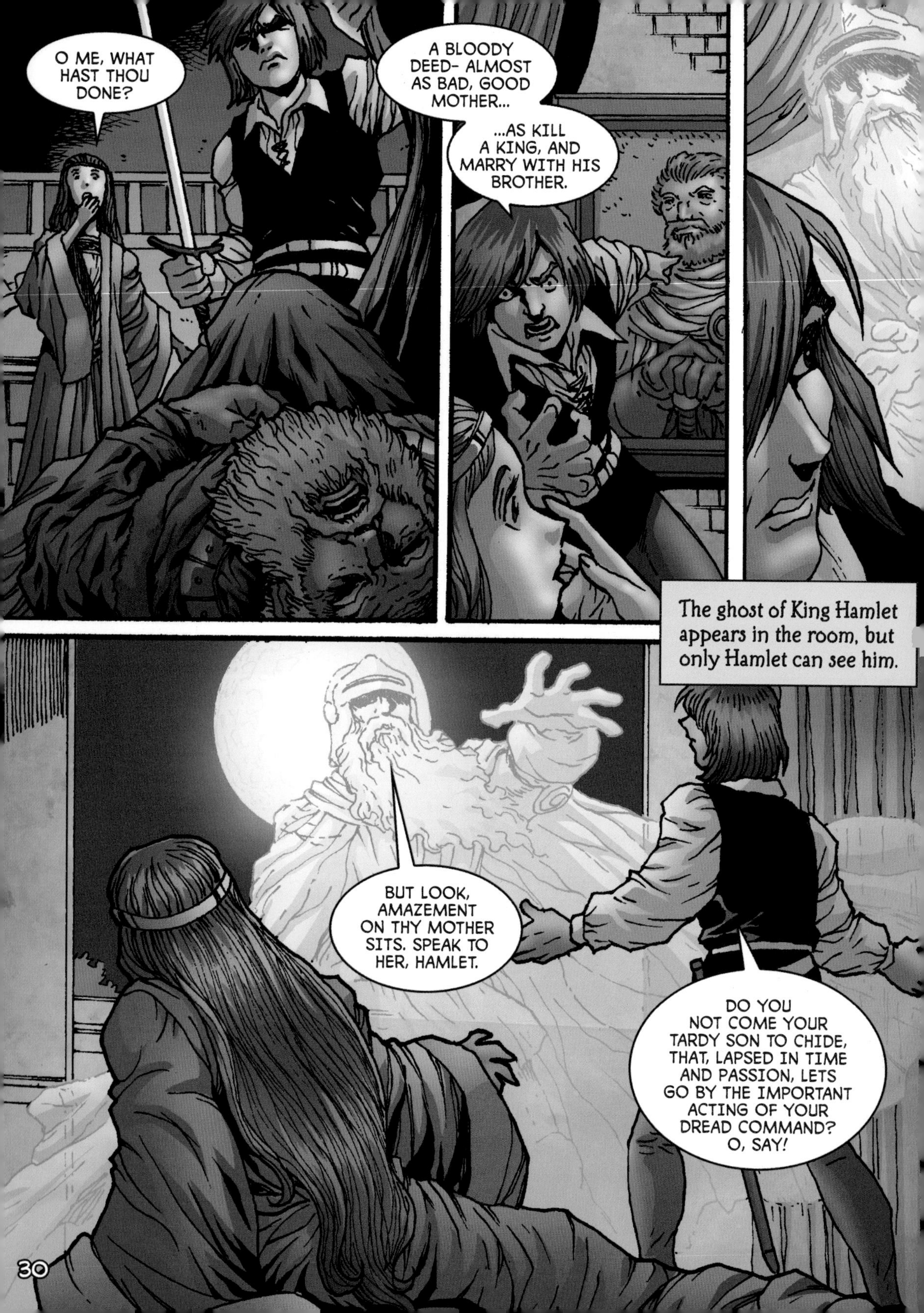
O ME, WHAT HAST THOU DONE?
A BLOODY DEED- ALMOST AS BAD, GOOD MOTHER...
...AS KILL A KING, AND MARRY WITH HIS BROTHER.
The ghost of King Hamlet appears in the room, but only Hamlet can see him.
DO YOU NOT COME YOUR TARDY SON TO CHIDE, THAT, LAPSED IN TIME AND PASSION, LETS GO BY THE IMPORTANT ACTING OF YOUR DREAD COMMAND? O, SAY!
BUT LOOK, AMAZEMENT ON THY MOTHER SITS. SPEAK TO HER, HAMLET.

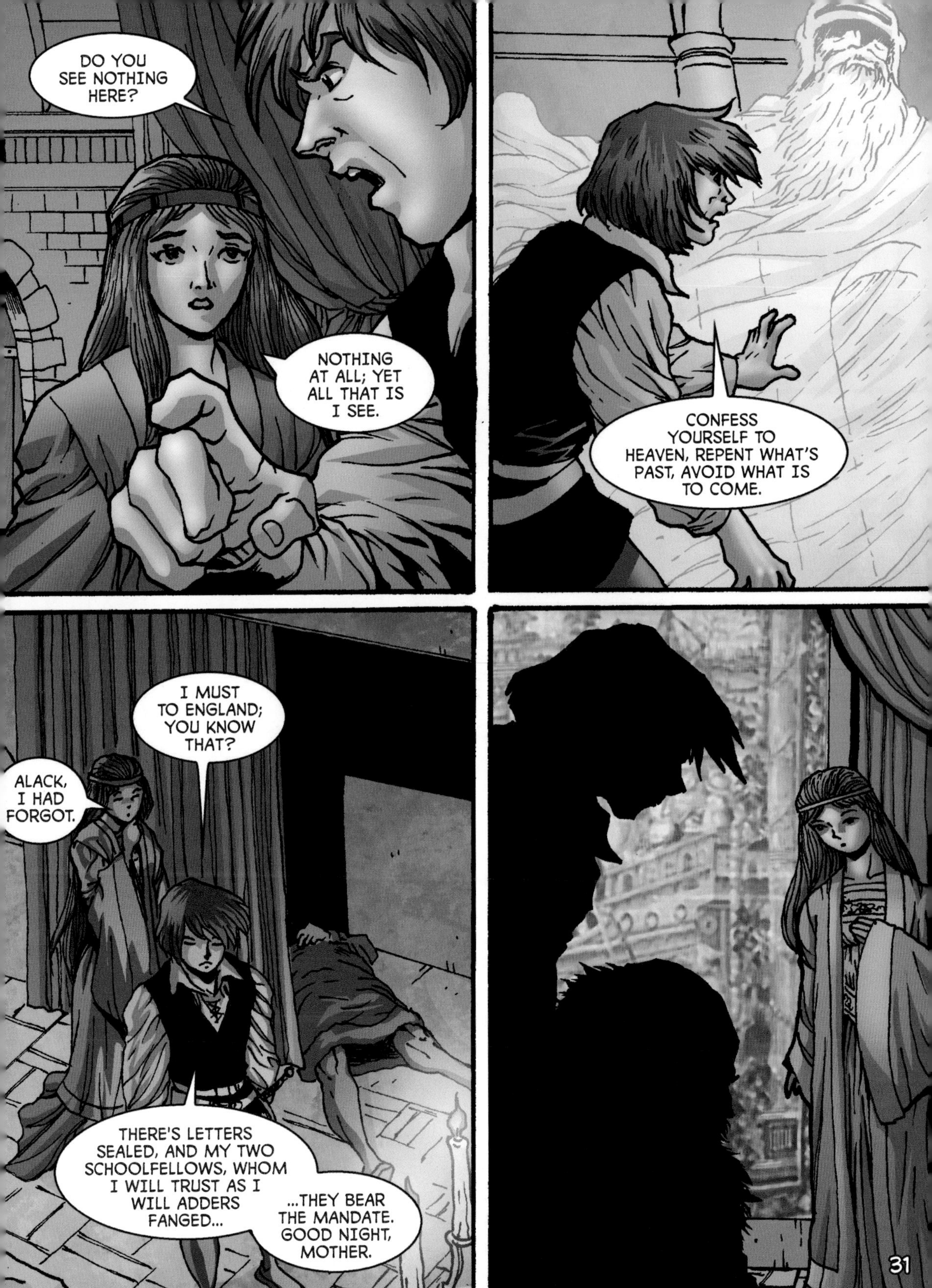
DO YOU SEE NOTHING HERE?
NOTHING AT ALL; YET ALL THAT IS I SEE.
CONFESS YOURSELF TO HEAVEN, REPENT WHAT'S PAST, AVOID WHAT IS TO COME.
I MUST TO ENGLAND; YOU KNOW THAT?
ALACK, I HAD FORGOT.
THERE'S LETTERS SEALED, AND MY TWO SCHOOLFELLOWS, WHOM I WILL TRUST AS I WILL ADDERS FANGED...
...THEY BEAR THE MANDATE. GOOD NIGHT, MOTHER.

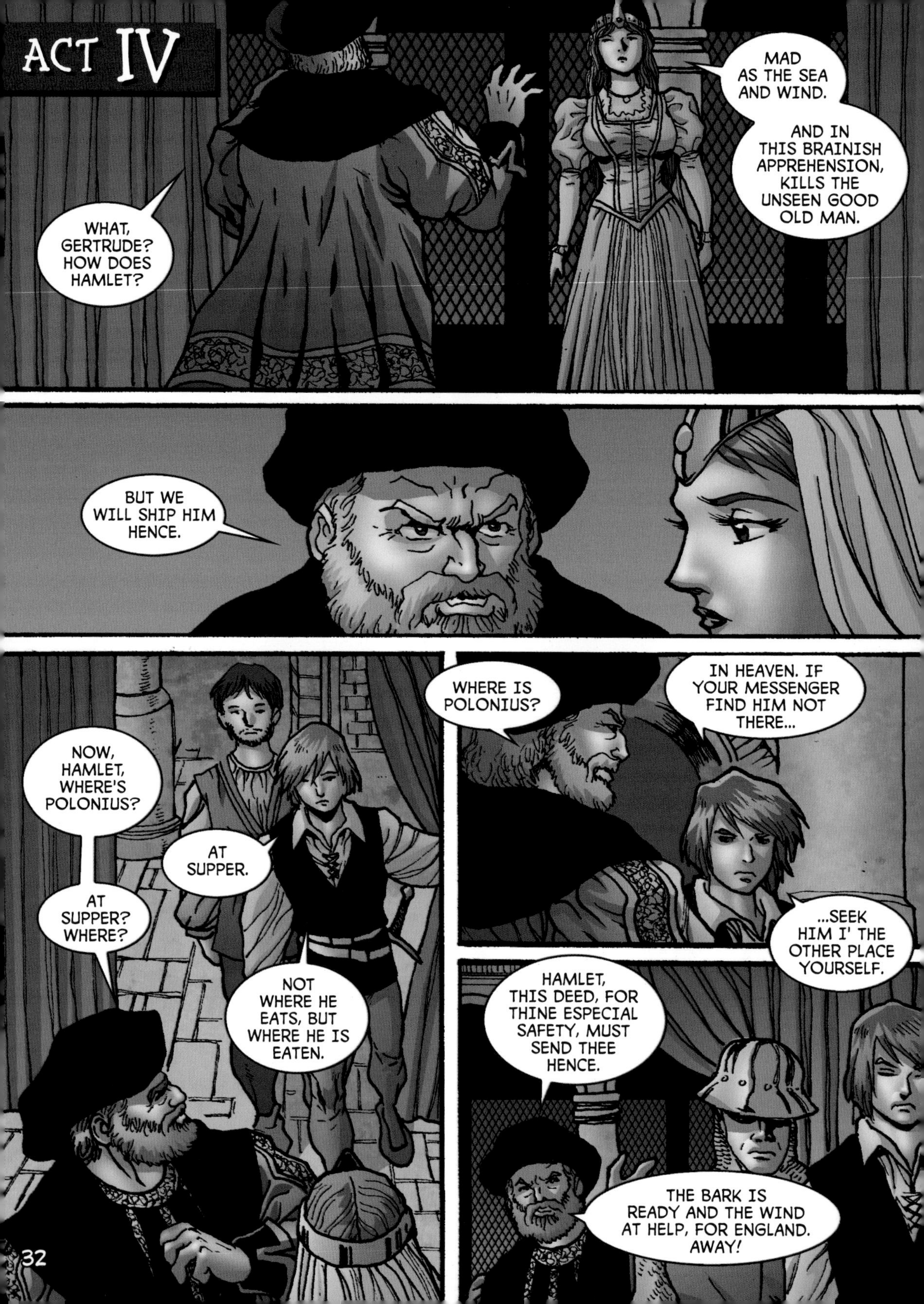
ACT IV
WHAT, GERTRUDE? HOW DOES HAMLET?
MAD AS THE SEA AND WIND.
AND IN THIS BRAINISH APPREHENSION, KILLS THE UNSEEN GOOD OLD MAN.
BUT WE WILL SHIP HIM HENCE.
NOW, HAMLET, WHERE'S POLONIUS?
AT SUPPER.
AT SUPPER? WHERE?
NOT WHERE HE EATS, BUT WHERE HE IS EATEN.
WHERE IS POLONIUS?
IN HEAVEN. IF YOUR MESSENGER FIND HIM NOT THERE...
...SEEK HIM I' THE OTHER PLACE YOURSELF.
HAMLET, THIS DEED, FOR THINE ESPECIAL SAFETY, MUST SEND THEE HENCE.
THE BARK IS READY AND THE WIND AT HELP, FOR ENGLAND. AWAY!

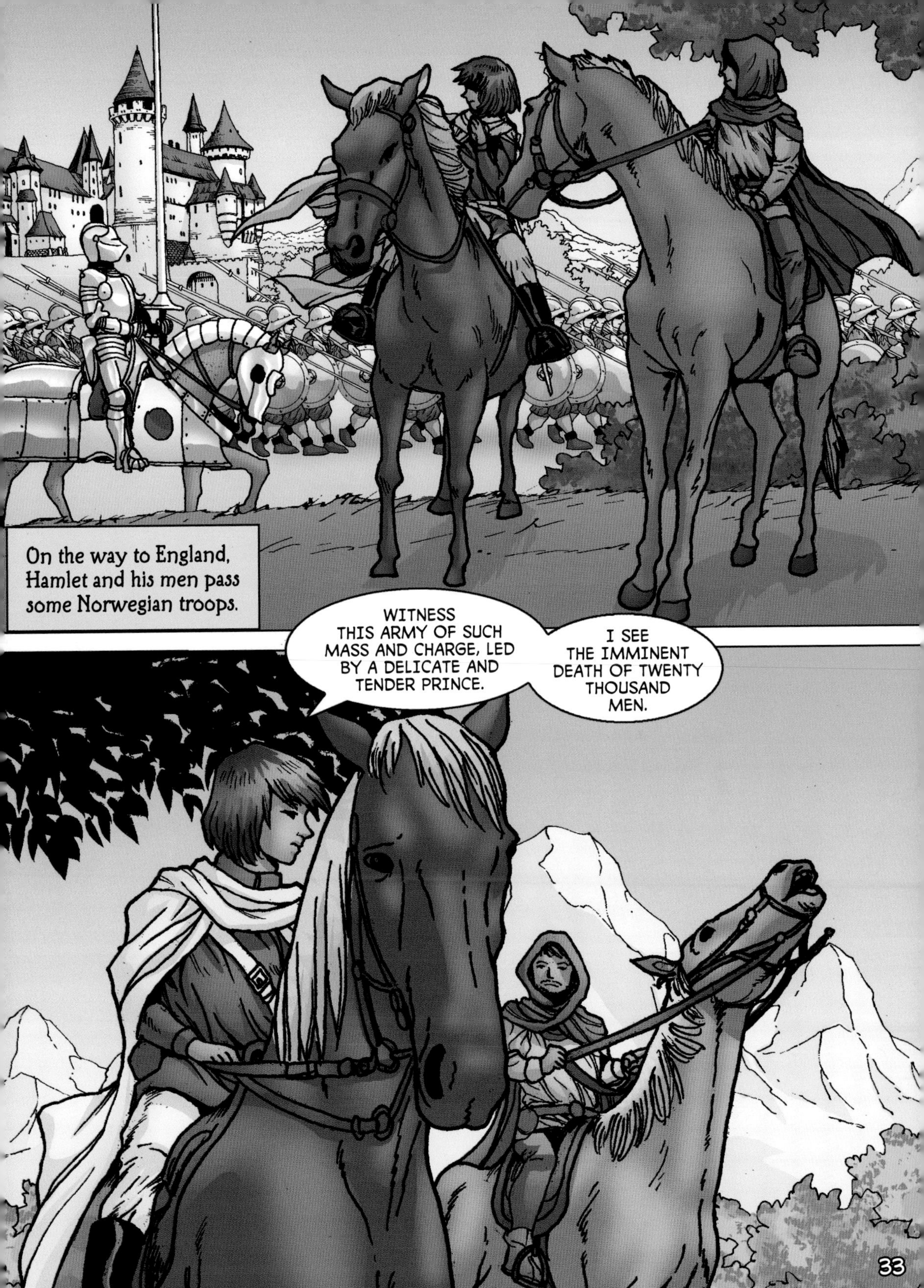
On the way to England, Hamlet and his men pass some Norwegian troops.
WITNESS THIS ARMY OF SUCH MASS AND CHARGE, LED BY A DELICATE AND TENDER PRINCE.
I SEE THE IMMINENT DEATH OF TWENTY THOUSAND MEN.

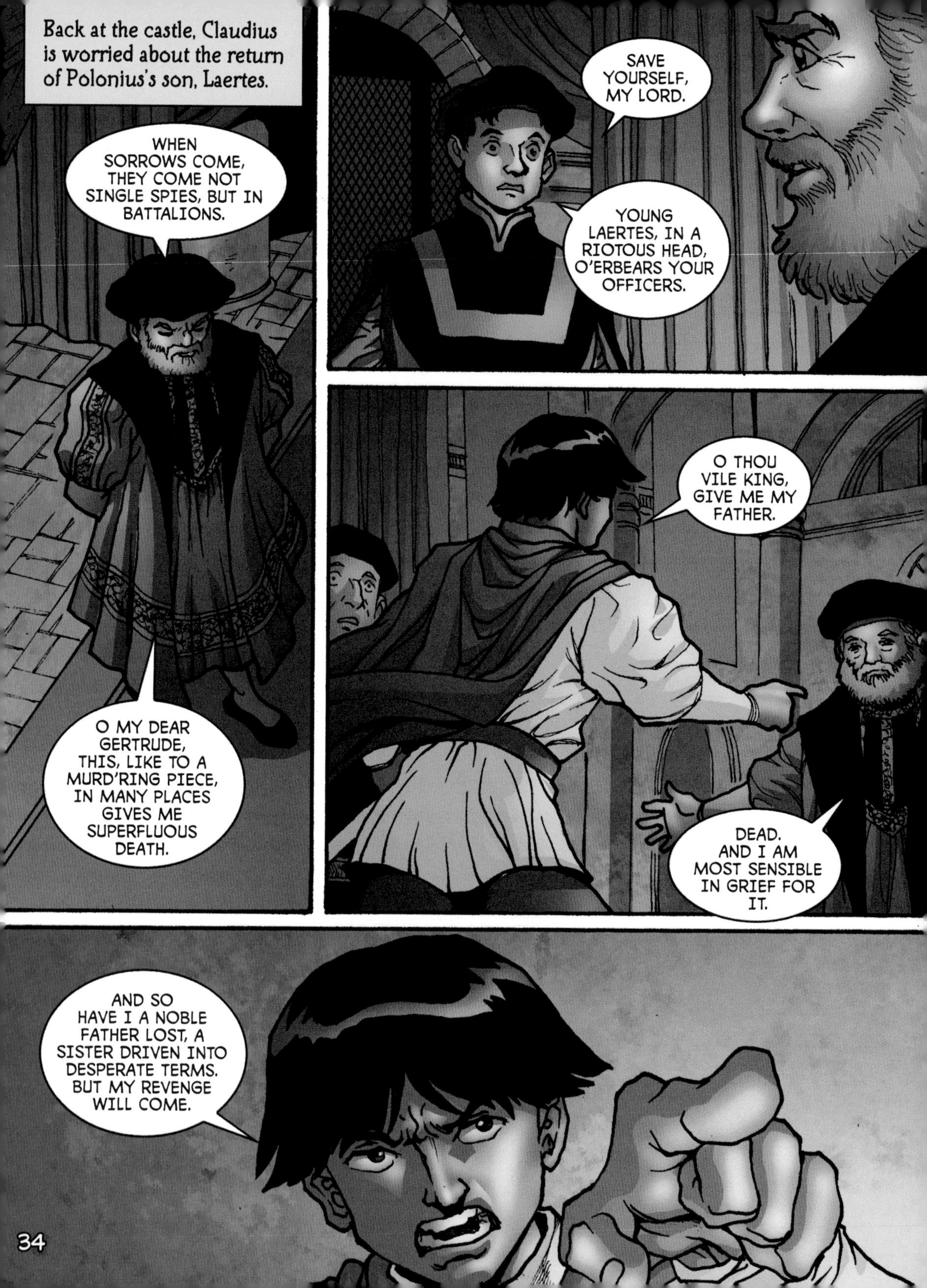
Back at the castle, Claudius is worried about the return of Polonius's son, Laertes.
WHEN SORROWS COME, THEY COME NOT SINGLE SPIES, BUT IN BATTALIONS.
O MY DEAR GERTRUDE, THIS, LIKE TO A MURD'RING PIECE, IN MANY PLACES GIVES ME SUPERFLUOUS DEATH.
SAVE YOURSELF, MY LORD.
YOUNG LAERTES, IN A RIOTOUS HEAD, O'ERBEARS YOUR OFFICERS.
O THOU VILE KING, GIVE ME MY FATHER.
DEAD. AND I AM MOST SENSIBLE IN GRIEF FOR IT.
AND SO HAVE I A NOBLE FATHER LOST, A SISTER DRIVEN INTO DESPERATE TERMS. BUT MY REVENGE WILL COME.

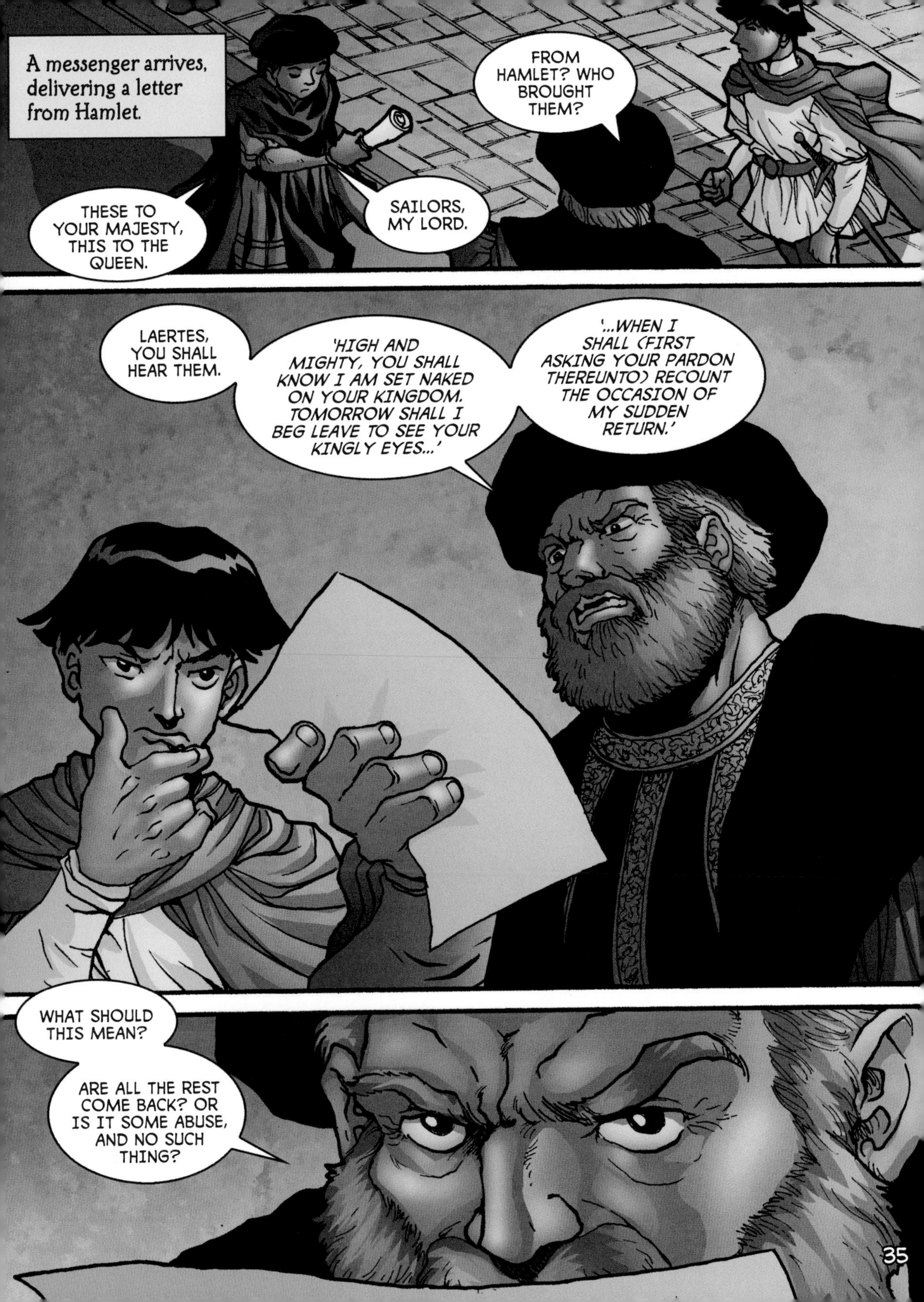
A messenger arrives, delivering a letter from Hamlet.
THESE TO YOUR MAJESTY, THIS TO THE QUEEN.
FROM HAMLET? WHO BROUGHT THEM?
SAILORS, MY LORD.
LAERTES, YOU SHALL HEAR THEM.
'HIGH AND MIGHTY, YOU SHALL KNOW I AM SET NAKED ON YOUR KINGDOM. TOMORROW SHALL I BEG LEAVE TO SEE YOUR KINGLY EYES...'
'...WHEN I SHALL (FIRST ASKING YOUR PARDON THEREUNTO) RECOUNT THE OCCASION OF MY SUDDEN RETURN.'
WHAT SHOULD THIS MEAN?
ARE ALL THE REST COME BACK? OR IS IT SOME ABUSE, AND NO SUCH THING?

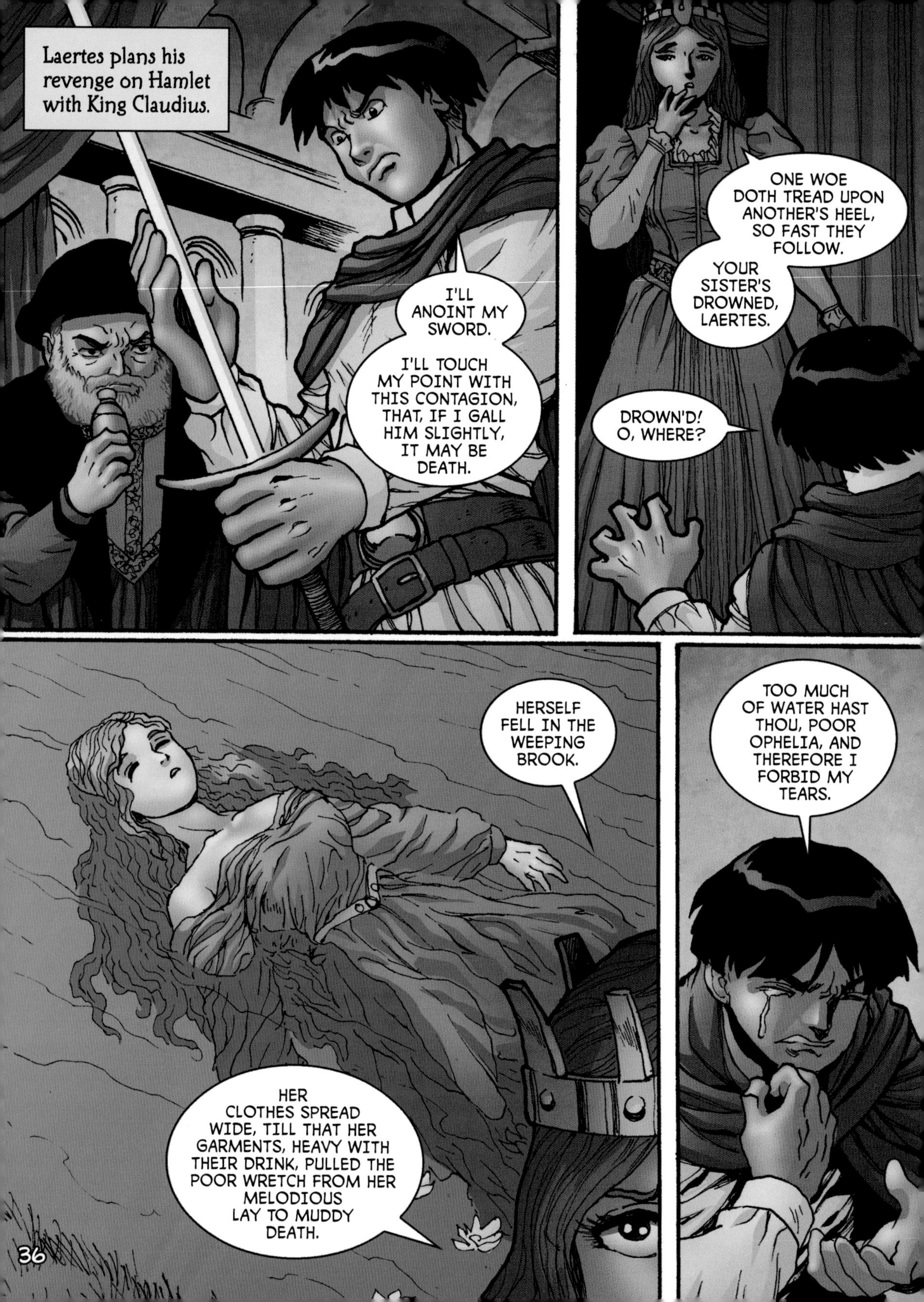
Laertes plans his revenge on Hamlet with King Claudius.
I'LL ANOINT MY SWORD.
I'LL TOUCH MY POINT WITH THIS CONTAGION, THAT, IF I GALL HIM SLIGHTLY, IT MAY BE DEATH.
ONE WOE DOTH TREAD UPON ANOTHER'S HEEL, SO FAST THEY FOLLOW.
YOUR SISTER'S DROWNED, LAERTES.
DROWN'D! O, WHERE?
HERSELF FELL IN THE WEEPING BROOK.
HER CLOTHES SPREAD WIDE, TILL THAT HER GARMENTS, HEAVY WITH THEIR DRINK, PULLED THE POOR WRETCH FROM HER MELODIOUS LAY TO MUDDY DEATH.
TOO MUCH OF WATER HAST THOU, POOR OPHELIA, AND THEREFORE I FORBID MY TEARS.

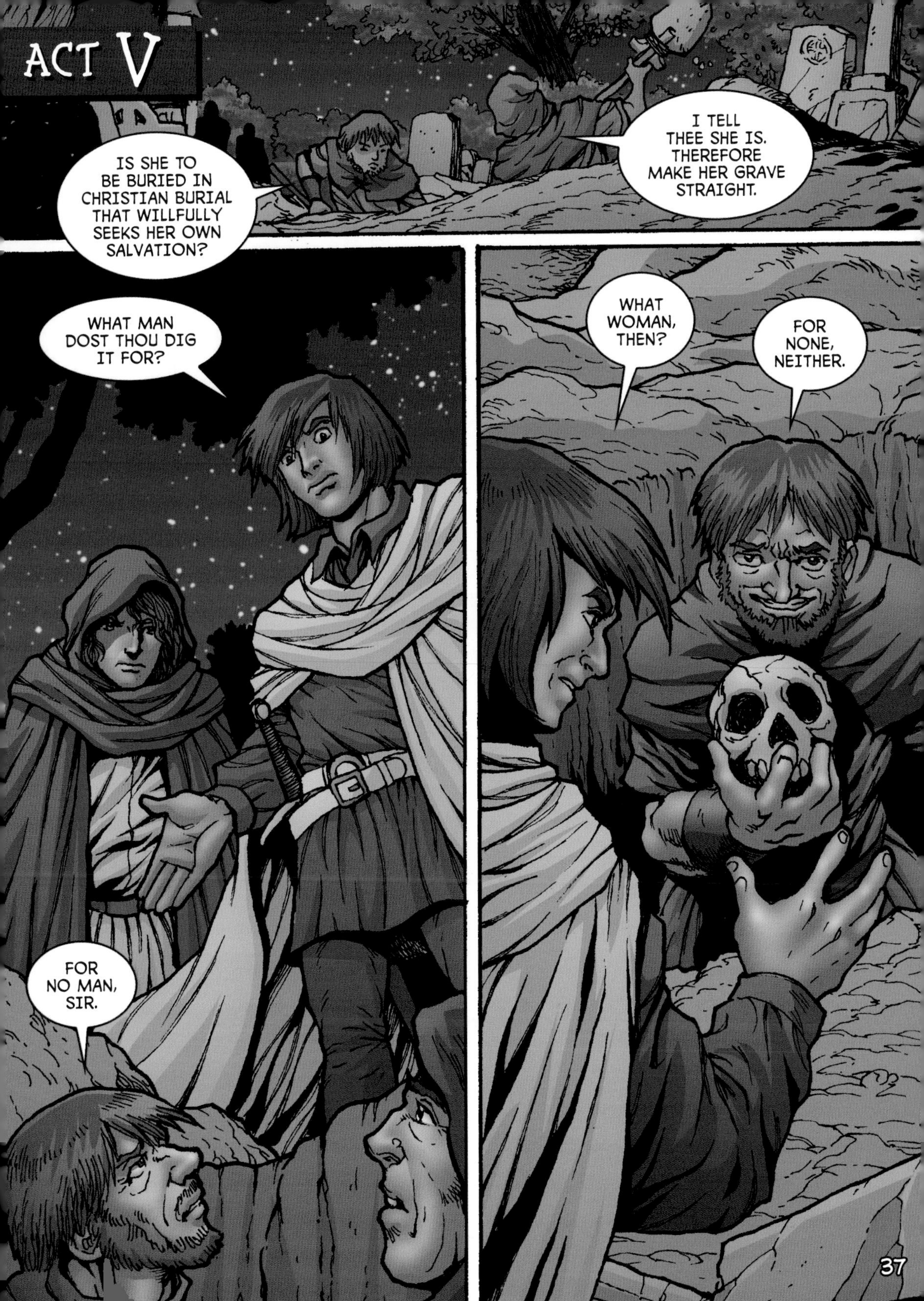
ACT V
IS SHE TO BE BURIED IN CHRISTIAN BURIAL THAT WILLFULLY SEEKS HER OWN SALVATION?
I TELL THEE SHE IS. THEREFORE MAKE HER GRAVE STRAIGHT.
WHAT MAN DOST THOU DIG IT FOR?
FOR NO MAN, SIR.
WHAT WOMAN, THEN?
FOR NONE, NEITHER.

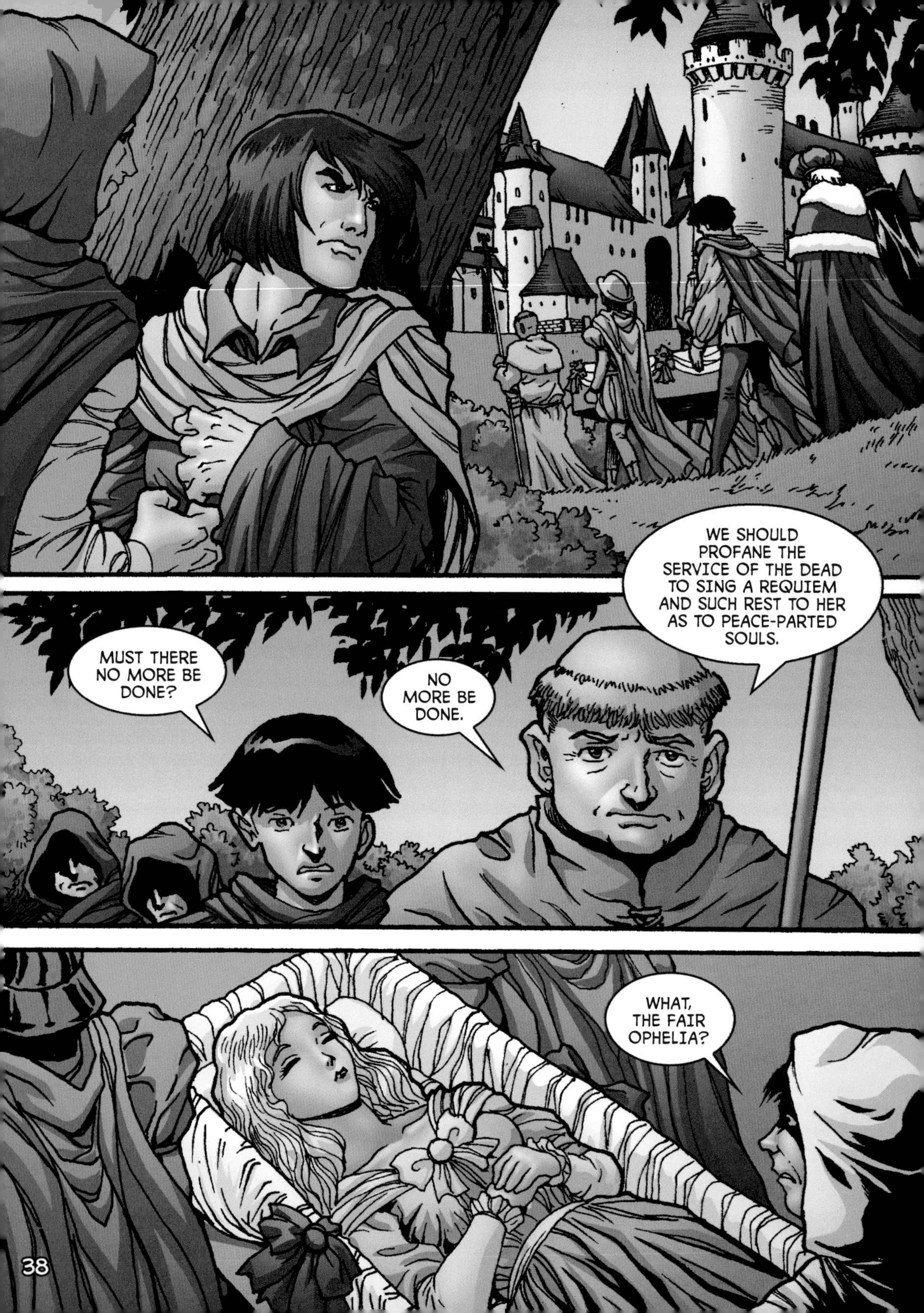
MUST THERE NO MORE BE DONE?
NO MORE BE DONE.
WE SHOULD PROFANE THE SERVICE OF THE DEAD TO SING A REQUIEM AND SUCH REST TO HER AS TO PEACE-PARTED SOULS.
WHAT, THE FAIR OPHELIA?

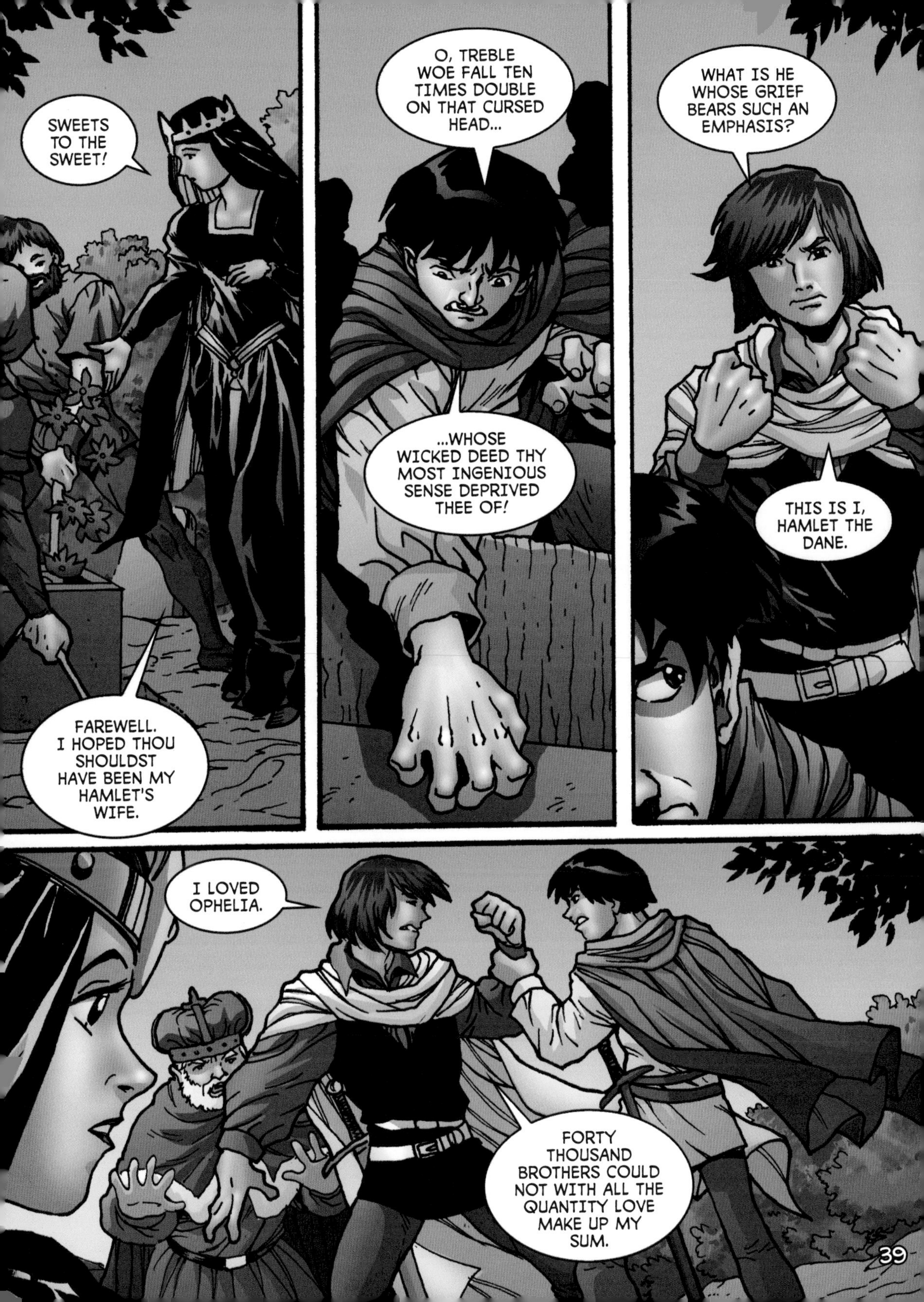
SWEETS TO THE SWEET!
FAREWELL. I HOPED THOU SHOULDST HAVE BEEN MY HAMLET'S WIFE.
O, TREBLE WOE FALL TEN TIMES DOUBLE ON THAT CURSED HEAD...
...WHOSE WICKED DEED THY MOST INGENIOUS SENSE DEPRIVED THEE OF!
WHAT IS HE WHOSE GRIEF BEARS SUCH AN EMPHASIS?
THIS IS I, HAMLET THE DANE.
I LOVED OPHELIA.
FORTY THOUSAND BROTHERS COULD NOT WITH ALL THE QUANTITY LOVE MAKE UP MY SUM.

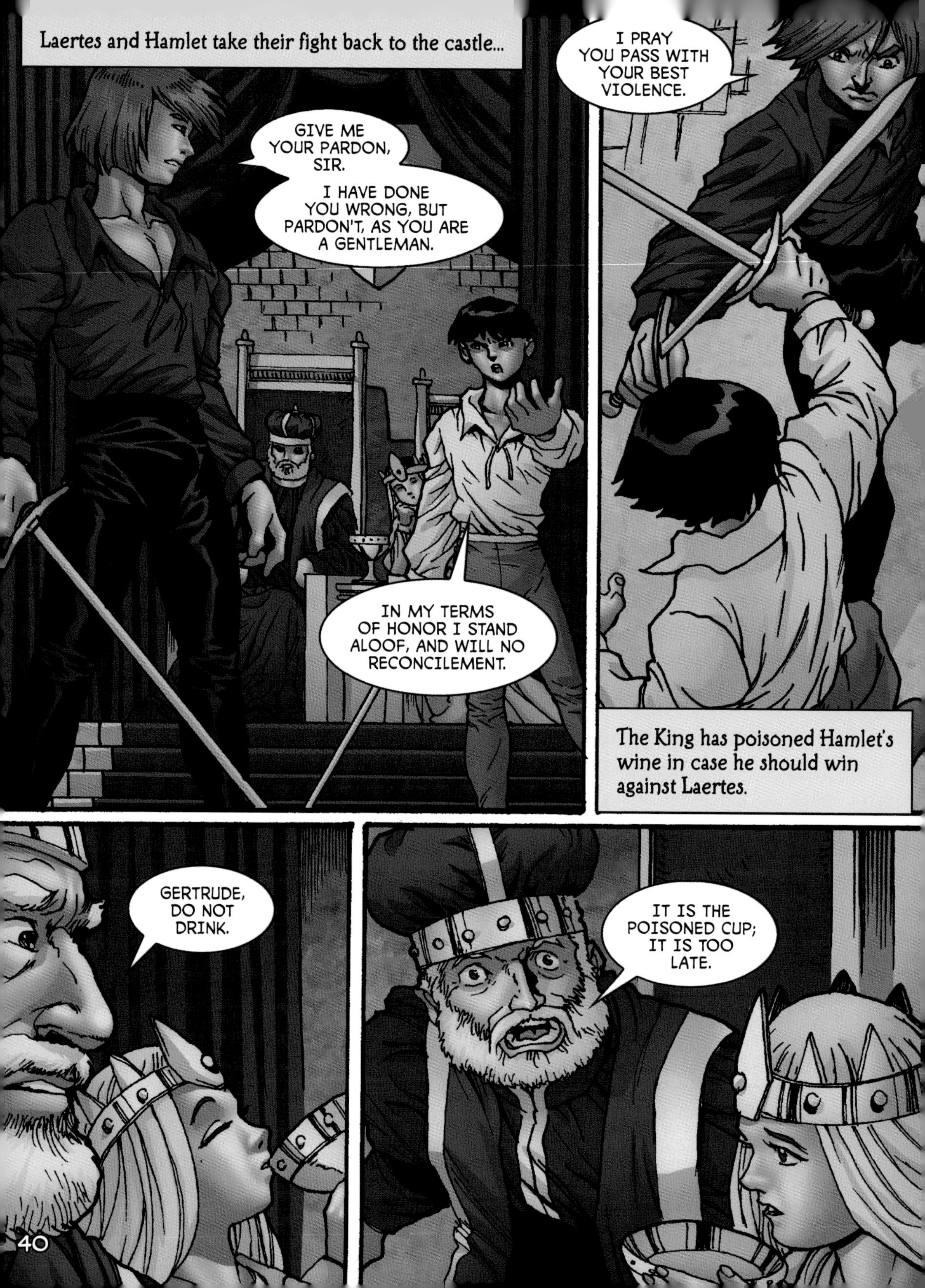
Laertes and Hamlet take their fight back to the castle...
GIVE ME YOUR PARDON, SIR.
I HAVE DONE YOU WRONG, BUT PARDON'T, AS YOU ARE A GENTLEMAN.
IN MY TERMS OF HONOR I STAND ALOOF, AND WILL NO RECONCILEMENT.
I PRAY YOU PASS WITH YOUR BEST VIOLENCE.
The King has poisoned Hamlet's wine in case he should win against Laertes.
GERTRUDE, DO NOT DRINK.
IT IS THE POISONED CUP; IT IS TOO LATE.

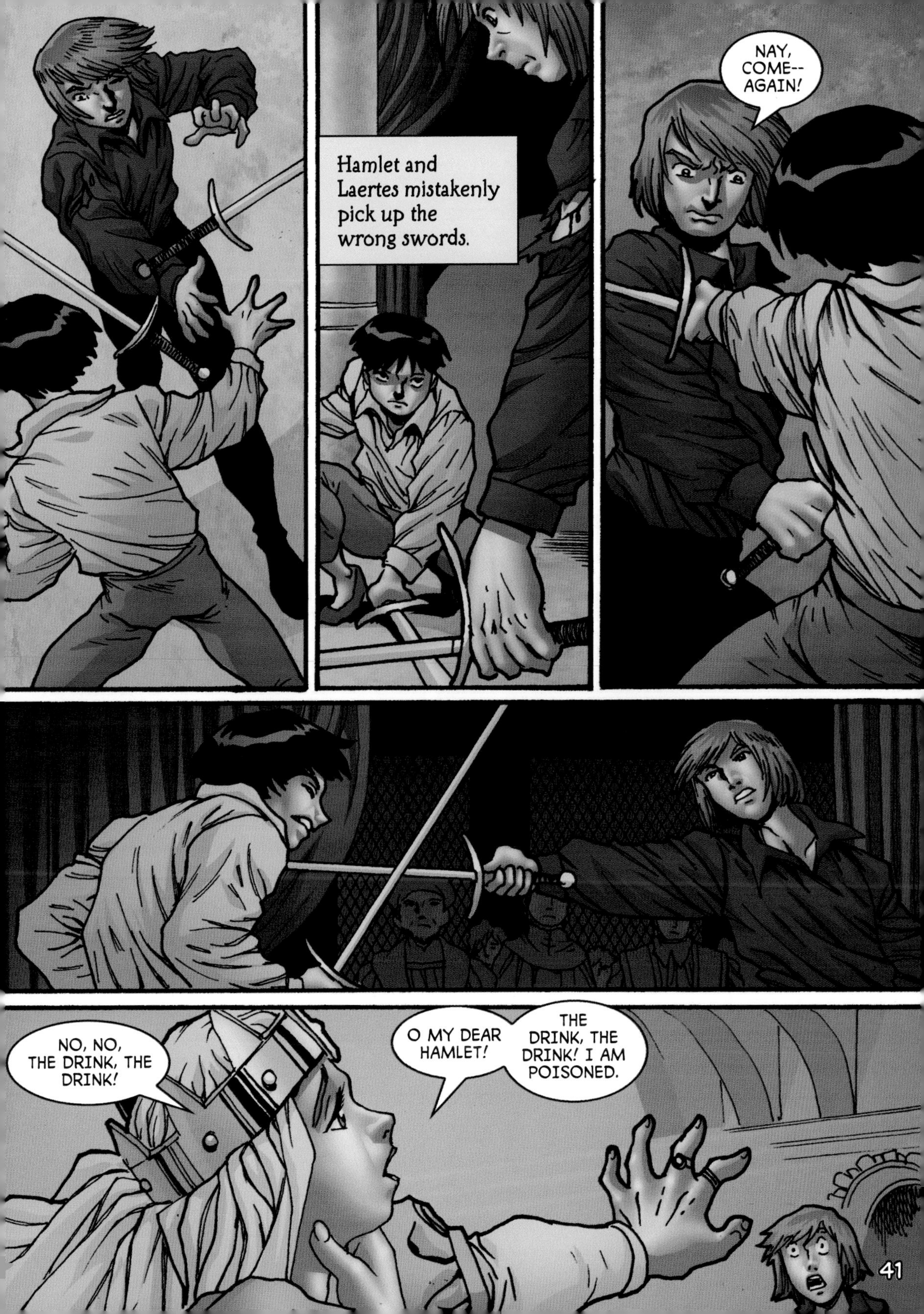
Hamlet and Laertes mistakenly pick up the wrong swords.
NAY, COME-- AGAIN!
NO, NO, THE DRINK, THE DRINK!
O MY DEAR HAMLET!
THE DRINK, THE DRINK! I AM POISONED.

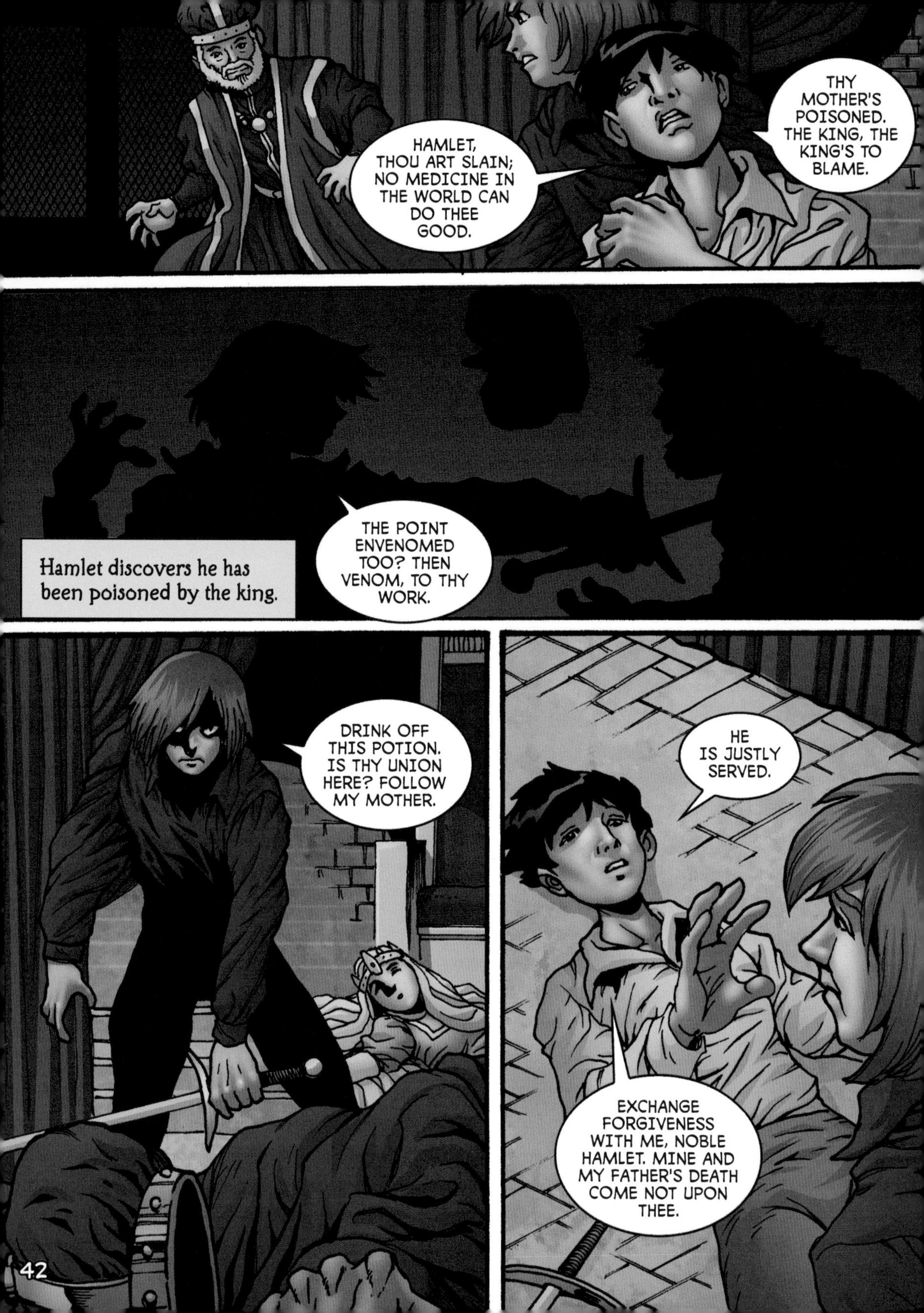

HAMLET, THOU ART SLAIN; NO MEDICINE IN THE WORLD CAN DO THEE GOOD.
THY MOTHER'S POISONED. THE KING, THE KING'S TO BLAME.
Hamlet discovers he has been poisoned by the king.
THE POINT ENVENOMED TOO? THEN VENOM, TO THY WORK.
DRINK OFF THIS POTION. IS THY UNION HERE? FOLLOW MY MOTHER.
HE IS JUSTLY SERVED.
EXCHANGE FORGIVENESS WITH ME, NOBLE HAMLET. MINE AND MY FATHER'S DEATH COME NOT UPON THEE.

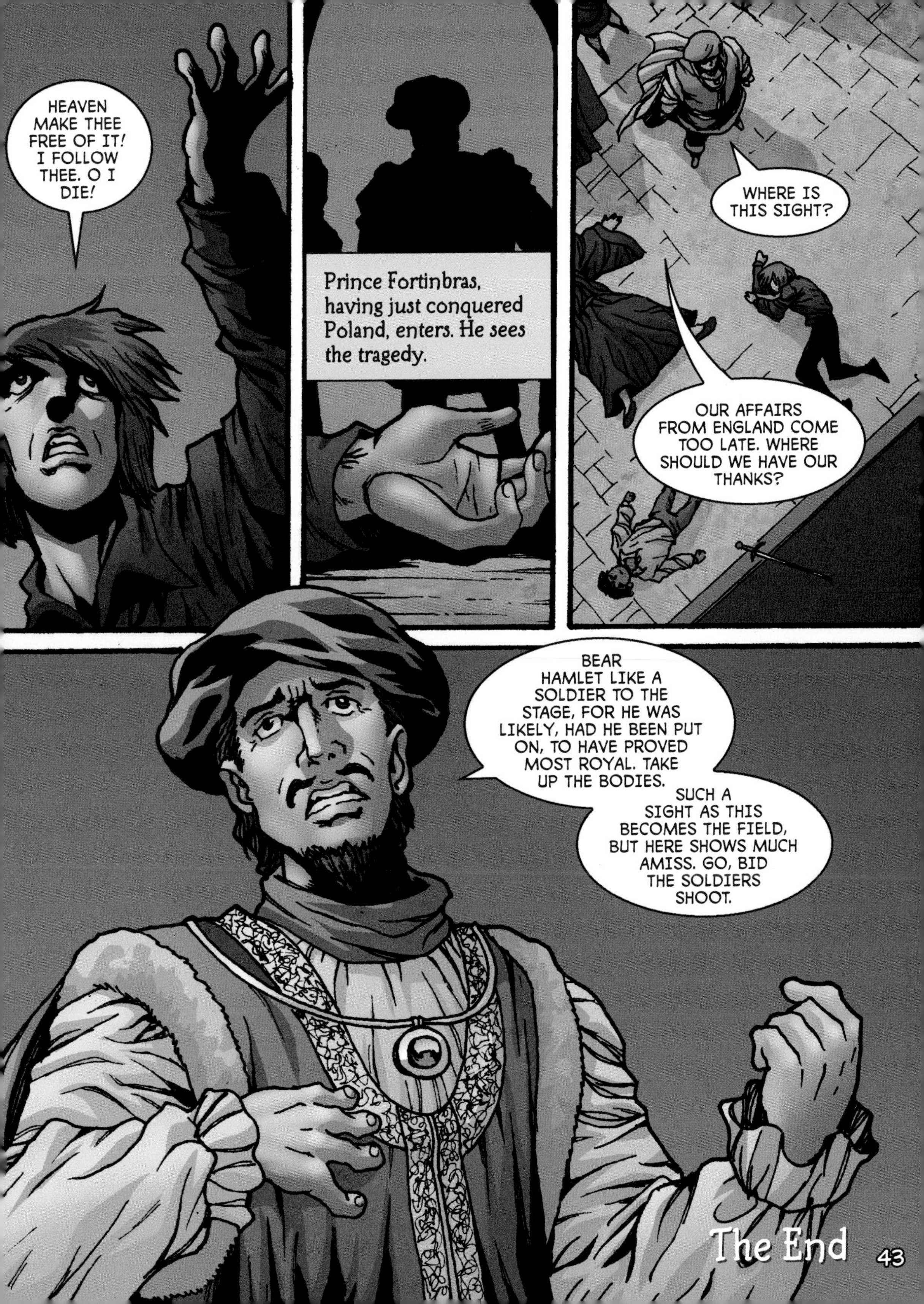
HEAVEN MAKE THEE FREE OF IT! I FOLLOW THEE. O I DIE!
Prince Fortinbras, having just conquered Poland, enters. He sees the tragedy.
WHERE IS THIS SIGHT?
OUR AFFAIRS FROM ENGLAND COME TOO LATE. WHERE SHOULD WE HAVE OUR THANKS?
BEAR HAMLET LIKE A SOLDIER TO THE STAGE, FOR HE WAS LIKELY, HAD HE BEEN PUT ON, TO HAVE PROVED MOST ROYAL. TAKE UP THE BODIES.
SUCH A SIGHT AS THIS BECOMES THE FIELD, BUT HERE SHOWS MUCH AMISS. GO, BID THE SOLDIERS SHOOT.
The End

# Discussion Questions

1. *Hamlet* is one of Shakespeare's tragedy plays. The tragedies have sad endings, often brought about by a personality flaw in the main character. What is Hamlet's fatal flaw? How did that contribute to the play's ending?

2. This play includes many characters who are seeking revenge. What lesson on revenge can you draw from the story? What evidence from the play supports this lesson?

3. Hamlet's apparent mental illness in the play is a subject of much discussion. Is he really going "mad," or is he simply faking it to fool Claudius and disguise his real plan? Or maybe it is some of both. What do you think, and why?

4. Hamlet's apparent mental instability surprises and worries his family members and friends. Do you think they respond well? Have you or someone you know had challenges like this following a loss? What happened? How did you handle it?

5. Why do you think *Hamlet* is still popular today, more than 400 years after it was written?

# Fun Facts

- Shakespeare wrote *Hamlet, Prince of Denmark* from about 1599 to 1601. It was first published in 1603.

- *Hamlet* is Shakespeare's longest play. His shortest is *The Comedy of Errors*.

- Because there are several sources of the text for *Hamlet*, there isn't one "correct" version of the play.

- It is possible Shakespeare based *Hamlet* on a story from a history of Denmark written by Saxo Grammaticus in the 1100s.

- In theater, Prince Hamlet is widely considered one of the most difficult roles to portray, partly because it is hard to tell whether he is faking his mental troubles.

# About Shakespeare

Records show William Shakespeare was baptized at Holy Trinity Church in Stratford-upon-Avon, England, on April 26, 1564. There were few birth records at the time, but Shakespeare's birthday is commonly recognized as April 23 of that year. His middle-class parents were John Shakespeare and Mary Arden. John was a tradesman who made gloves.

William most likely went to grammar school, but he did not go to university. He married Anne Hathaway in 1582, and they had three children: Susanna and twins Hamnet and Judith. Shakespeare was in London by 1592 working as an actor and playwright. He began to stand out for his writing. Later in his career, he partly owned the Globe Theater in London, and he was known throughout England.

To mark Shakespeare and his colleagues' success, King James I (reigned 1603–1625) named their theater company King's Men—a great honor. Shakespeare returned to Stratford in his retirement and died April 23, 1616. He was 52 years old.

# Famous Phrases

*The lady doth protest too much.*

*Something is rotten in the state of Denmark.*

*Take it to heart.*

*To thine own self be true.*

*To be, or not to be—that is the question.*

*When we have shuffled off this mortal coil.*

# Glossary

**arras** – a wall hanging.

**bark** – a small sailing ship.

**choler** – irritation, frustration, or anger.

**confound** – to confuse.

**contagion** – poison.

**doublet** – a man's jacket.

**fishmonger** – a person who sells fish.

**lunacy** – insanity or madness.

**perchance** – maybe; possibly.

**repel** – to push away.

**requiem** – a song of grief.

**surmise** – to form an idea based on little or no evidence.

# Additional Works by Shakespeare

**Romeo and Juliet (1594–96)**

**A Midsummer Night's Dream (1595–96)**

The Merchant of Venice (1596–97)

Much Ado About Nothing (1598–99)

**Hamlet (1599–1601)**

Twelfth Night (1600–02)

**Othello (1603–04)**

**King Lear (1605–06)**

**Macbeth (1606–07)**

The Tempest (1610-11)

- *Bold titles are available in this set of Shakespeare Illustrated Classics.*

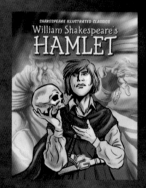

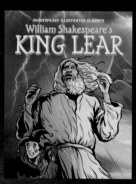

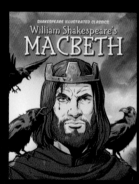

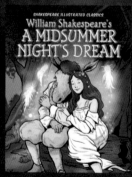

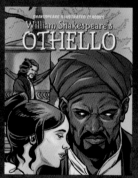

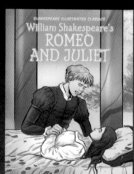

SHAKESPEARE ILLUSTRATED CLASSICS
William Shakespeare's
HAMLET

SHAKESPEARE ILLUSTRATED CLASSICS
William Shakespeare's
KING LEAR

SHAKESPEARE ILLUSTRATED CLASSICS
William Shakespeare's
MACBETH

SHAKESPEARE ILLUSTRATED CLASSICS
William Shakespeare's
A MIDSUMMER NIGHT'S DREAM

SHAKESPEARE ILLUSTRATED CLASSICS
William Shakespeare's
OTHELLO

SHAKESPEARE ILLUSTRATED CLASSICS
William Shakespeare's
ROMEO AND JULIET